Hush-Hush

A Village Library Mystery, Volume 4

Elizabeth Spann Craig

Published by Elizabeth Spann Craig, 2020.

HUSH-HUSH

First edition. December 1, 2020.

Written by Elizabeth Spann Craig.

Chapter One

I'd just finished eating a pretty messy lunch of leftover spaghetti in the library's staff lounge when I felt someone staring at me. I glanced down and, sure enough, Fitz the library cat was staring intently at me, a clear message in his green eyes.

"Can't reach my lap, buddy?" I asked, scooting back away from the breakroom table. But Fitz didn't seem to want to jump onto me.

"How about if I join you on the floor?" I murmured, glad I'd had the foresight to wear slacks today. I was also glad I was wearing khaki slacks and not black ones that Fitz's orange and white fur would have shown up on.

I grabbed my book and settled with my back to the wall. Fitz, happy now, leapt into my lap and immediately curled up into a ball for a nap.

Fortunately, I was using my e-reader and could rub Fitz with one hand and flip "pages" with the other. After a fairly steady diet of shocking and twist-filled psychological thrillers over the past few weeks, I was happy to return to a classic and one of my favorites: *The House of Mirth* by Edith Wharton. There wasn't a whole lot of mirth going on in the book, but it was still an excellent read, as always. I looked at the clock and confirmed I had fifteen more minutes left of my lunch break before I needed to head back out to the library circulation desk.

It seemed like no time at all had gone by before the door to the breakroom flew open and the room was besieged. At least, it *felt* as if it had been besieged. The reality was there was a woman who'd entered and it was no longer just Fitz and me, reading on the floor while a sunbeam filtered over my legs from the window.

The woman, our new librarian, Ellie who'd been with us for about a month, seemed to be in her own little world . . . a world that involved getting a Slim-Fast shake from the breakroom fridge. She whipped out her phone when it started ringing and said in a husky voice, "Hi there. Still on for lunch? Great. See you then."

I was starting to feel very awkward on the floor and it wasn't just because my legs were going to sleep with Fitz napping on them. Ellie clearly hadn't spotted me yet, but I supposed she wasn't used to looking on the floor for lunching librarians. I cleared my throat.

Ellie shrieked and jumped back, which startled the sleeping Fitz into rearing up, fur standing on end, spitting and hissing. This further made Ellie shriek and throw her Slim-Fast, which fortunately wasn't open yet.

I put my hand on my heart and Ellie did the same.

"Sorry for scaring you," I said.

Ellie seemed to be trying to catch her breath. Her blonde hair still looked perfect, but her sky-blue eyes were open wide.

"Oh my gosh," she said breathlessly. "I did *not* expect anyone to be on the floor. Ohh, is Fitz okay?"

Fitz was a very laid-back cat, but he still looked rather alarmed. He calmed down and seemed pacified when Ellie reached out an apologetic hand to him. He bumped his orange head against it, purring his rough purr.

The last thing I wanted to do after a restful lunch break was spend the remaining minutes with Ellie. There was nothing really *wrong* with Ellie, but there were some oddities about her. Considering her profession, she was inordinately chatty and didn't seem to take a hint and be quiet if a patron (or co-worker) was reading or studying. I also had the feeling Ellie could be incredibly snoopy. I'd seen her listening intently to patron conversations on the other side of a bookcase when she was shelving . . . pausing dramatically in her task and really focusing on what the people were saying. I'd taken phone calls before and was positive Ellie was listening in to my one-sided conversation before quickly doing something else when I'd turned around.

On the upside, I was relieved to have another full-time librarian on staff. My coworker Luna and I had been putting in a lot of hours before she was hired. The library was a busy one and when our director, Wilson, hired Ellie, it took a lot of the pressure off.

"Fitz is fine," I said with a smile to Ellie. "You know how cats are—they're easily spooked."

She giggled. "Maybe I'm a cat then. I've been kind of jumpy lately."

I stood up and slid my e-reader into my purse. "I should get back to it. How are things going out there?"

Ellie shrugged. "Pretty quiet, actually. That's why I thought I'd go ahead and grab something to drink for a few minutes."

"I'll leave you to it, then. Looks like Fitz is settling down with you, too."

Fitz had snuggled up against Ellie's leg as she rubbed him. I headed out of the breakroom, cutting my lunch break a bit short but saving myself from further conversation with Ellie.

Luna, my orange-haired (this week) coworker noticed. She came over from the children's section, frowning. "You're not taking a full lunch break? Are you insane?"

I chuckled. "Maybe. I know the afternoon is probably going to be busy." I nodded over to indicate the breakroom door. "Ellie was in the lounge, so I decided to cut things a little short."

Luna made a face. She was far from Ellie's number one fan. "Then I totally understand it. To think I tried to be friends with her!"

I shrugged. "Maybe we aren't giving her enough of a chance. She might grow on us."

"Like poison ivy," said Luna. "She's *impossible* to be friends with."

"Which is saying something, considering you're outgoing and so easy to make friends with. Ellie simply must not be trying."

Luna had tried to take Ellie under her wing when she started at the library. But every kind gesture Luna made was rebuffed by Ellie. Not only that, Luna overheard Ellie making snide comments on the phone about Luna's colorful and unique fashion sense.

We stopped talking as Ellie hurried back out of the break-room. She gave them a cheery smile. "Heading out to lunch. See you soon!" She disappeared out the sliding door.

Luna made a grumbling noise. "So she's heading for lunch ten minutes early. On *your* lunch break. If I didn't know better, I'd think she *planned* it that way—to drive you out of the break-room and then take part of your lunch when you're back at the circulation desk."

"Ellie should be grateful Wilson has been so distracted."

Luna chuckled. Her mother, Mona, had recently embarked on a new relationship with Wilson, and it was still in the delicate beginning stages. Wilson was such a stickler for punctuality that it was lucky for Ellie he'd been so consumed with the budding relationship.

"Yes, it's been interesting to see Wilson not completely on top of things," said Luna. "Have you noticed how casual he's gotten? In terms of his wardrobe, I mean?"

My eyes grew big. "Casual? Wilson?"

"That's right. Sometimes he doesn't wear a tie with his suit. Sometimes he wears a tie but no jacket. That's progress, right?" Luna grinned at me. Wilson's usual uniform was an immaculate suit and well-polished shoes.

"I must not have been paying very close attention. Now I'll have to really look."

Luna nodded behind me. "Well, you're about to get your chance. Here he comes now."

Wilson walked over to join us, frowning vaguely as we both smiled at him. "You two look like Cheshire cats."

I saw Wilson was indeed wearing a navy-blue blazer, khaki pants, and a bright white shirt. This, for Wilson, was quite casual indeed.

"Inside joke," said Luna breezily.

"Is your mother coming in today?" asked Wilson to Luna.

"Of course. There's film club." Luna quirked an eyebrow at him. "I understand you're going to be the one presenting this time?"

Wilson put a hand up to pull at his non-existent tie. "Yes. Yes, that's right." He paused. "I was thinking perhaps film club wouldn't have much of a turnout. You know, with the rain and everything."

Was Wilson a little nervous about presenting the film? He did tons of public speaking in front of what was high society for Whitby, North Carolina. It surprised me he could be anxious about appearing in front of any group. But then, if Mona was there, it wasn't really just *any* group.

Luna said, "Low turnout? At film club?" She glanced over at me. "Ann, isn't film club usually packed?"

"We have a group of avid regulars who really try to make every meeting." I shrugged. "That's not to say that there couldn't be a day with unusually low turnout." But I seriously doubted it.

Wilson looked a bit deflated.

Luna put her hands on her hips. "I don't totally understand, Wilson. Are you *hoping* there won't be many people here? Because that doesn't make sense. It doesn't sound very library-di-rector-ish."

Wilson waved his hand in the air in dismissal. "No, no, of course not. I want all of our library programs to flourish. I suppose I just want this event to go especially well since Mona was so excited about my heading up the group today. As a guest." There seemed to be a slight emphasis on *guest* as if he was making a point that this would most likely be a one-time thing.

I said, "I'll go in there and get everything in the community room set up for you."

"Oh, you don't have to do that," said Wilson, although his eager expression belied his words.

"It's fine—I do it every time so it's practically muscle memory now. What movie did you choose for the group?"

Wilson said, "*2001: A Space Odyssey.*"

I nodded and said, encouragingly, "That's right. Classic movie." Inside, though, I had the feeling Mona was going to be either exceedingly confused during the film, or possibly pull her knitting out in the middle of it. It was definitely one of those slow-build movies . . . visually amazing, but complex.

Wilson said, "I did poll a few of the film club members when they came out of the meeting last month and asked if they'd seen the movie. Only one of them had."

I grinned. "Let me guess. Timothy had."

"That's the young man who attends, isn't it?" asked Wilson.

I nodded.

"Yes, he was the one."

Timothy was our youngest, but most avid member. He was a gangly teen who was able to make our meetings because he was homeschooled. He had a big, warm grin and always got along really well with our group. Plus, he was pretty much an expert when it came to films, having watched a wide range. He also seemed to like reading up on them.

"Well, I'm sure he'll love watching it again and the rest of the gang will enjoy seeing it for the first time. It's supposed to be Kubrick's masterpiece, after all," I said.

Wilson brightened at this, although there was still just the smallest wrinkle of concern between his brows.

"Would you like me to moderate the meeting along with you?" I suggested slowly.

He brightened again but then shook his head. "Ordinarily, that would probably make the facilitation a lot easier but the truth is I completely forgot about the class this afternoon that I said I'd help teach. It popped up as a reminder on my computer a few minutes ago and is actually the reason I was looking for you."

A class he was sure to ask me to teach. One I hadn't prepared for. This afternoon was going from bad to worse. "Sure," I said, trying to infuse my voice with a little enthusiasm. "What's the class on?"

"You won't have to prepare, don't worry. It's an introduction to Word. I'd meant to bring in Frank Morrison to handle it so I could just do a short intro and leave the class up to him, but I completely forgot."

This was all very un-Wilson-like, which was proof again that Mona had really flustered him, and not all in a good way. Plus, people who took intro to Word classes tended to need a lot more help with computers than the ordinary user.

"No problem," I said with a tight smile.

Wilson gave me a relieved grin in response. "Perfect. All right then, I guess I better practice what I'm going to say about the film. See you in a bit."

As he headed off, I went into the community room to set things up in there for film club. This involved pulling out chairs, getting the computer set up to show and project the movie, and pulling the popcorn machine out of the storage closet and getting it ready.

Then there was a flurry of activity at the circulation desk as all the parents and toddlers from Luna's storytime came up to check out board books and picture books of all persuasions.

Luna walked up to me after the crowd dissipated. "All right, now I'm ready for *my* lunch break and it sure would be nice to see Ellie coming back in right around now."

I glanced at the clock. "So she left early and is coming back late. Nice."

"Ugh. Wilson only seems to pay attention when *I'm* the one doing stuff like this. So annoying." She wandered over to the door and looked out. She turned around to stare at me, eyes wide. "She's back."

"Well, it's not *that* shocking," I said. "Ellie was going to eventually return if she wanted to keep her job."

"Yes, but she's getting out of someone else's car. A *man's* car."

I shrugged as I wiped down the circulation desk with a wipe. "She's allowed to date. I'd be surprised if she *didn't* date."

"Yeah, but this is a married man. Ted Griffith! I went to high school with him and he's been married to Sunny since right after we all graduated." Luna hurried back toward me so she wouldn't be caught snooping as Ellie apparently started walking toward the library. Luna affected a bored, waiting look as Ellie came in.

"Glad you're here. I'm starving," said Luna pointedly.

Ellie gave her a breezy smile. "Well, go have some lunch. You're allowed."

"Unfortunately, my break is going to be cut a little short since you're back late. Part of the time I have to pick up my mom and bring her to the library for film club, so . . ." Luna shrugged and narrowed her eyes at Ellie.

Apparently, you really couldn't beat around the bush at all with Ellie. She was either going to completely ignore it or wasn't capable of picking up on social cues. "Okay, well, tell her I said hi," said Ellie breezily. "I'm gonna head over and do some shelving."

Luna growled under her breath as Ellie practically skipped over to a cart filled with books and disappeared into the stacks. "I have a funny feeling about her shelving."

I grinned at her. "Oh, give her a break, Luna. She only uses shelving as an excuse to be on her phone *some* of the time."

Luna made a face. "That's what I suspected. Okay, I better get out of here before I really start fuming."

The next forty-five minutes were quiet at the library, which was good since I had an unexpected class to teach. I looked up some tips on teaching Word and came up with a couple of handouts that the students could take home with them. I checked out the signup for the class and was surprised to see there were fifteen people enrolled. That was quite a lot for a library tech class, at least at our branch.

When Luna returned from lunch with her mother in tow, Mona waved at me and came over to say hi. Luna seemed preoccupied with something going on in the parking lot behind her.

"It's Sunny Griffith," she hissed at me as she hurried up.

"Who?" I asked.

"Sunny. She's Ted's wife. Plus, she's just made it on the library board of trustees. Remember, I was telling you they've been together since we were all at high school together? I wonder if she saw Ellie and her husband together?"

"Drama at the library," I said dryly.

Luna intoned, "Here she comes."

Chapter Two

I n came a middle-aged woman with blonde hair carefully pulled back in a chignon. Her clothes were obviously expensive but in a very nothing-to-see-here way: monotone beige. She quickly glanced around the library as she came in, as if she were looking for something . . . or someone.

"Can I help you?" I asked politely while Luna caught her breath.

Sunny gave me a smile, but it was the kind of smile that looked as if she were baring her teeth. "Thanks, but I'm just here to pick up a couple of holds. I thought I might stick my head in and speak to Wilson for a moment—is he in?"

Luna nodded and I said, "He's in his office right now." Wilson's office door was *always* open for a library trustee, even if he *was* cramming for film club.

Sunny gave me a smile again, this time a bit more genuine. "Great." She reached out a hand and shook Luna's and mine. "I'm Sunny Griffith. I'm new on the library board."

"Good to meet you," Luna and I chorused.

Sunny strolled off, but decidedly not in the direction of the holds.

"I think she's looking for Ellie," breathed Luna.

"If she is, it's none of our business," I said firmly. I tried to look back at the handout I was proofing for the class, but my eyes were drawn back to the sight of Sunny meeting up with Ellie. Ellie had her sweetest of expressions on and appeared to be asking Sunny if she needed any help. Sunny gave her a coolly dismissive look and stalked off toward Wilson's office, leaving Ellie staring after her. When Ellie glanced up and saw Luna and me gaping at her, she quickly disappeared into the stacks again.

"Curiouser and curiouser," said Luna.

"Yes, it is," I said, "but look, I've *got* to finish getting ready to teach this computer class in a few minutes. Plus introduce Wilson at the film club before the class starts."

"Got it," said Luna, giving me a salute. "Work now, gossip later." She hurried off to the children's section.

I finally finished up the handouts and had a rough idea of how I was going to talk about using Word to the computer class. I saw a couple of people walking into the computer area and I greeted them and told them I'd be there in just a few minutes and put the handouts in a stack. Then I walked over to the community room.

Wilson, who'd managed to slip away from his impromptu meeting with Sunny, joined me a couple of minutes later. Mona was already in there, beaming with pride at Wilson being the presenter for the day. Wilson looked as ill at ease as he had earlier.

Timothy, my favorite club member, was enthusiastically talking up the film, waving his gangly limbs around as he spoke. "It's a slow starter, but it's so *beautiful*. And really moving, too."

Wilson gave him a grateful look. He definitely needed someone in his corner for this movie, which could be inscrutable. He was still looking a bit nervous as to the movie's reception by the group, but not as fidgety as he had been before.

I introduced Wilson, everyone gave him a polite round of applause, and then I excused myself and ducked back out to the computer class.

There was a motley assortment of students in the class when I arrived. There were seniors, as I'd expected, but there was also a teen in the room, which surprised me. There were also a couple of middle-aged women who said they'd never really used Word to its fullest capability and they wanted to learn more.

The range of ages and abilities definitely gave me pause. I took a quick survey to find out where everyone was with their computer savviness. There was an older man who said he barely knew how to turn a computer on and he didn't understand what "right click" meant. The teen, when pressed, said she was trying to get better with Word for the papers she was starting to get assigned—she seemed to be looking for tips on formatting and setting up page breaks and numbered pages. I felt my palms sweating.

"Okay," I said, thinking quickly, "I was going to go with a lecture-style format where I covered the basic functions of Word, but now I'm thinking it might be more beneficial for everyone if I just worked with you in small groups."

I rearranged everyone so the most inexperienced users were in one group and the students who wanted to learn tips and tricks were in another. I had everyone introduce themselves so they'd hopefully have something to talk about amongst themselves while I was helping the other group. Fortunately, it seemed like a really amiable and chatty group of people. I gave a sigh of relief over that. Plus, it looked like the girl who was attending for formatting assistance was able to help a couple of the other patrons.

I was relieved when the hour was finally up and everyone seemed satisfied with what they'd gotten from it.

"Thanks, everybody, for coming," I said with a grin to the class, expecting everyone to quickly disperse and get back to whatever they were doing before they came to the computer class. I was hoping I could head over and watch the remainder of film club and see how people were enjoying the movie.

But apparently, that wasn't quite in the cards yet. An older lady raised her hand and said, "You know what I really need? Maybe not a formal class in a particular program. I mean, you did a fantastic job today getting everyone what they need. But what would really help for me is sort of a general computer help hour where I could just drop in with my phone or my laptop or my tablet and get help with whatever thing I need. Not just Word, but other things, too."

Another patron chirped up. "Me, too. Sometimes I get so frustrated because I can't open a website on my computer."

The older lady nodded at him. "Sometimes I get locked out of my email because of my password being wrong and I can't figure out how to get back in."

I said, "So you're saying a kind of drop-in clinic for computer problems would help you out the most?"

Even the teenager nodded.

I said cautiously, "That does sound like something the library could consider helping out with. I could run it by my director."

"Would you be the one helping at the clinic?" asked the older lady in sort of a pleading tone. "Sometimes other people get frustrated when I don't understand computer stuff, but you're pretty patient and seem to know what you're doing."

Taking on something else at the library, especially on a regular basis, was probably the last thing I needed right now. But I said, "Let me speak with my director first and see what he says. But if you signed in on the sign-in sheet, I can keep you updated with any developments for a clinic."

Everyone filed out and I finally hurried over to the community room to see how film club was faring. Mona had a crinkled brow, but at least she hadn't pulled her knitting out. Timothy was looking completely engaged and absorbed in the movie. The rest of the film club members seemed to be engrossed in the film, Wilson included (although, by his own calculations, he'd watched the movie at least ten times).

It's not a short film, so I had to pop out a couple of times to make sure everything was going all right in the library. We had more volunteers than usual, so everything looked under control.

Finally, it was film discussion time. Wilson walked slowly to the front of the room and gave everyone a fairly anxious glance, his gaze alighting on Mona last. She still had that pucker of confusion on her face. "So, what did everybody think?" he asked.

"Fantastic!" said Timothy, bouncing his lanky body in his seat. He looked as if he might have grown an inch since the last time I saw him, which had only been a few weeks ago.

Mona pursed her lips. "I wasn't so sure what was going on with the apes, but I liked the part with the computer trying to murder people."

Wilson made a half-hearted attempt to try and explain the scene with the apes at the beginning of the film, but he couldn't seem to really get through to her and Mona looked even more confused.

Timothy raised his hand as if he were in a classroom and Wilson called on him exactly as if he were a professor. "May I?" Timothy asked and Wilson nodded.

Timothy launched into an explanation of the dawn of mankind and how the obelisk in the picture figured in. Mona tilted her head to one side, frowning at first before slowly nodding.

Wilson's brow wrinkled as he said, "Does that all make sense?"

"In a manner of speaking, I suppose it does. I'm also not sure about the baby at the end." Mona gave him an apologetic look. "It's the kind of movie I have to watch a second time to really understand. But then, I even got confused with the Star Wars movies, and children seemed to be able to follow all the storylines with those." She shrugged and added with a smile, "Maybe you could come over one night and we can watch the film again."

Wilson blushed.

George, a burly regular who owned the typewriter repair shop on the square, chimed in. "What I'd really like to talk about, and what I thought was fascinating, is the subject of artificial intelligence. When did this movie come out again? Late 60s?"

Wilson nodded and carefully double-checked the notecards he held. "1968."

George continued, "I think it's pretty amazing that Kubrick was prescient enough to see how computers and AI could be dangerous for humans." Speaking as a man who worked daily and very closely with typewriters, George had a perhaps understandable enmity with computers.

This launched an entire discussion on artificial intelligence and the future of humanity. Wilson looked pleased and rather proud throughout.

Fifteen minutes later, the club broke up and members scattered out into the library to find books or pick up their holds—most of them were huge readers as well as film fans. Timothy stayed for a few minutes to help me stack the chairs back up and hesitantly said, in a carefully offhanded manner, "So . . . it looks like you have a new librarian here."

I glanced up and noticed his cheeks were pink. I smiled at him. "We do! Ellie Norman is her name and she's been helping us out for a few weeks now."

"You probably really needed the extra help, didn't you?" asked Timothy. "I mean, it's always so busy in here."

"We sure did need it. Still could use some extra hands now, as a matter of fact."

Timothy said in that same carefully casual way, "My mom was trying to encourage me to get some volunteer hours in . . . you know, they look good for college applications and help other people out, too. I looked into a variety of different things, but

I kept remembering the library is one of my favorite places to come. Maybe I could help out here?"

"Definitely! You'd be a great volunteer." I meant it, too. He was a smart kid and got along well with adults, which boded well for mixing with the patrons. His motives might have been a little questionable (and might have involved a crush on Ellie Norman), but I knew he would be fabulous.

"What kinds of things do library volunteers do here?" he asked.

"Oh, there's a lot of stuff . . . it's not just shelving books. You can help us pull requested items and put them on hold shelves for patrons, help with the summer reading club, make display boards, and maybe even help with our study buddies program." I stopped, my eyes opening wide. "Hey, don't I remember that you're excellent with computers?"

He blinked at me in his owlish way. "Computers? Sure. What do you need . . . programming? Help making the library site secure?"

"Actually, I was thinking about something completely different. I've got to run it by Wilson, but we may be running computer help clinics for patrons who are stumped by things happening on their different devices."

Timothy chuckled. "That happens to be my specialty."

"Do you have a lot of patience? Because it's the kind of volunteering that might tap out your reserves. These are patrons who may not know really basic computer terms and might be totally overwhelmed easily." I felt the need to warn him. He was so young and a complete computer native. It might even be hard for him to imagine people who didn't know what a "window" or a "tab" were or felt unsure whenever they had to reboot their device.

"I help out my Nana all the time and it's no big deal at all. Believe me, I can handle it."

I grinned at him. "Then the job is yours if it all gets approved by Wilson. I'll be in there to help you out too since I'm not sure how many people will show up. I was thinking it would be better if we use the clinics as more of a teaching opportunity than just fix the patrons' issues ourselves."

"Sort of like that old saying: *Give a man a fish and you feed him for a day. Teach him to fish and you feed him for a lifetime*?" asked Timothy.

"Exactly. Maybe then they'll be able to have the confidence to work through some of their own issues when they come up."

Timothy hurried to catch up with George and I caught up with Wilson on the way out. "Hey, great job!" I said.

Wilson looked pleased. "You think so? I was a little worried a couple of times that the movie was losing people."

"Oh, you know. Maybe they were lost for a few minutes, but then the film moved on to something else and they caught on. Great pick—lots of good discussion this time."

"Did the computer class go all right?" asked Wilson.

"It did. It didn't go exactly as I'd planned, though, because everybody was on a different level. I worked with small groups instead. Then I ended up with a patron request for a specific library-sponsored event."

Wilson raised his eyebrows. "Another class?"

"Not really—more of a drop-in clinic." I explained it to him and also said that Timothy had expressed an interest in volunteering for it.

"Good, good," said Wilson brusquely. "Just be sure to mention it a lot on social media. I'll arrange extra coverage for the library those days in case you get tied up at the clinic with Timothy. Maybe I can also ask Frank Morrison to help out. I need to call him anyway because we have the one desktop that's still on the blink."

Frank was one of the tech guys who helped out with IT and photocopier issues at the library. He was a big, blustery guy who seemed to me to have a borderline hot temper.

I said, "That's fine, but I'm not sure he's going to be ideal for the clinic. He doesn't seem like he'll have the patience to work with some of the tech-challenged patrons. Plus, we'd have to pay him for his time. Timothy would be working for free and I know he's supposed to be excellent with electronics."

Wilson considered this and then said, "Good point. The last thing we want is for somebody to represent the library poorly. I'll speak to Frank about the desktop, but I'll leave out the part about the clinic."

I locked up the community room after everyone had left and headed back out into the library. I was doing some research for a patron who'd called in to ask for more information about their unusual health problem when the sliding doors opened and I saw Ellie's sister, Pris walk in. She seemed very unlike Ellie in every way. Where Ellie was fair and lively, Pris was dark and serious. I'd met her a couple of times since she was not only an enthusiastic reader herself, but often came in to get picture books for her daughter. She was separated from her husband, shared custody of her young daughter, had a court date for the divorce, and was actively looking for employment. She'd been living with Ellie since she'd moved to Whitby. Pris looked a little flushed and I spotted a bicycle parked right outside the library doors.

I called out a greeting and she came up to the research desk with a smile. "Good to see you, Ann. Where's Mr. Fitz today?"

I chuckled. "He's likely in a sunbeam somewhere. You should track him down . . . he's always up for a cuddle."

"And my sister?" she asked, her features clouding just a touch.

She didn't even really have to ask because Ellie had already spotted her and was storming over. Pris met up with her halfway and Ellie started letting her have it. I hopped back into my research, not wanting to get involved with a family argument. I did perk up, though, when I could clearly hear Ellie saying, "It's my turn to lock up tonight, so that's one reason."

As far as I was aware, it was *my* turn to lock up at the library. I glanced up and saw Ellie's face was set and stubborn. Pris whirled around and stormed out.

Ellie saw me looking in her direction and shrugged, walking over.

"Hey, I thought it was my night to close up here," I said lightly. I wasn't in the mood for Ellie to snap my head off and it looked like she might be in the frame of mind to do just that.

"Can we trade?" she asked. "The last thing I want is to hang out at home if I'm having a spat with Pris. Can I lock up tonight and you open up tomorrow morning?"

"Sure, that's fine." I looked at my watch. "I guess that means I'll be heading out of here soon."

"Yeah," said Ellie with another shrug. She was staring absently toward the door Pris had left through. She gave a short laugh. "Sorry about my thing with my sister. I guess once you get used to living on your own, it's just hard to adjust to having somebody else there."

I was surprised Ellie was opening up to me at all. She'd pretty much kept to herself the whole time she'd worked at the library. "Definitely. I've been on my own for so long that it would be a real challenge to get used to a roommate."

Ellie said, "We've been fine, but she's got a lot of stress right now and that's not helping. She's about to get divorced and Pris and her ex have been really scrapping over the custody issues." She made a face. "It's been pretty ugly. Pris doesn't have a job here yet, so that makes it tough, too. Her lawyer told her that she really needs to be employed before her court date but nobody has an opening. I have no idea how long she might be staying with me, but it's starting to look like it might be a while. Maybe I need to look for a bigger place."

Which was tough on a librarian's salary.

Ellie could apparently read my mind like I had a cartoon thought bubble outside my head. She snorted. "Yeah, we don't make a lot, do we? But I recently came into a little cash. A new place might just be in the works." She spotted Wilson and pivoted to head off into the stacks. "Thanks again for the trade," she called behind her.

Chapter Three

An hour or so later, I was walking out of the library along with Mona and Luna. Fitz was headed home with me, curled contentedly in his cat carrier.

Luna frowned at me. "For some reason I thought you were locking up tonight."

"I was. Ellie wanted to trade. Apparently, she needed a break from her sister."

Luna blew out a gusty sigh. "That Ellie! Pris is perfectly nice. I was actually thinking about spending some more time with her—maybe asking her to go out to a movie with Mom and me."

Mona made a face and said, "As long as it's not tonight. I'm still trying to process *2001: A Space Odyssey*."

"You liked it though, didn't you, Mom?"

"I *think* so," said Mona slowly, "although I need more time to absorb it all. There were definitely *parts* of it I liked. I definitely think I need to watch it a second time."

We said goodbye in the parking lot and I unlocked my car and carefully put Fitz's carrier in the backseat and buckled it in. Then I headed home, windows down, radio playing, and singing off-key to Adele. When I got back to my cottage, I noticed the flower beds were in dire need of some weeding. The extra hours at home were a gift, I decided, and one I didn't want to squander. I took Fitz in and fed him before sliding on my gardening gloves and setting to work with the weeding. Fitz bathed himself on the windowsill and then watched me through the window with interest.

"Hey there," came a deep voice and I jumped, deep in my thoughts.

It was Grayson Phillips, my neighbor and friend. He was also my perennial crush, who seemed completely unaware (determinedly unaware?) of my feelings. Recently, I'd been seeing more of him, although not really in the way I wanted. We appeared to be "buddies"—I wrote a monthly library column for the newspaper he edited and we'd hike together on local trails near Whitby. He managed to cheer me up no matter what kind of mood I started out in because he was relentlessly upbeat, handsome, kind, and witty. Although in the past, his very presence had turned me into a blathering idiot, I was able to put that aside now. Most of the time.

Grayson looked apologetic now. "Sorry I scared you."

I stood up, stretching in the process. "No worries. I was just focused on what I was doing, that's all."

Grayson glanced over at the window where Fitz was staring intently at him and chuckled. "Looks like Fitz is keeping an eye on you."

I snorted. "More likely he's trying to persuade you to come inside and scratch him under his chin for a while." Realizing I probably *should* invite him in, I quickly said, "Would you like to come in?"

He shook his head. "Actually, I was about to ask if you wanted to join me for a run."

He did indeed have athletic clothes on. I'd been trying not to notice how sculpted his body was underneath them. It was tempting, but the fact of the matter was that despite the fact that I needed to do more exercising, I was pretty wiped out.

"Can I take a raincheck on that jog?" I asked lightly. "It was kind of a busy day at work and I don't think I'd really be able to keep up." I brightened with an idea. "But if you wanted to stop by on your way back and have a glass of wine with me, I'd be up for that."

He grinned. "Here I am trying to be all healthy and you're tempting me with alcohol."

Well, I had to try to tempt him with something.

He said, "You're on. I'll be back in thirty minutes."

Yeah, I definitely wouldn't have been able to run for that long. I'd have ended up walking back home. I found myself whistling as I continued weeding the garden and shook my head at my transparency. After another twenty-five minutes I disposed of the weeds and went in to wash my hands and pour the wine right as Grayson returned.

He tapped on my front door and I greeted him with a glass. "Come on in," I said, stepping back so he could walk through the door.

He shook his head ruefully. "I'm way too sweaty to sit on your furniture. Do you mind if we take the wine outside?"

I didn't mind anything at all when I was hanging out with Grayson. I grabbed my own glass and joined him at a small wrought-iron table in a corner of the front yard garden. My great-aunt, whom I'd inherited the house from, had been quite a gardener and had thoughtfully planted perennials and flowering bushes which were riotous in true English garden fashion.

I waited for him to start up the conversation, because my typical conversation starters were rife with weather references, books, and my work at the library.

Fortunately, Grayson was a lot more outgoing than I was. "What was it like growing up in Whitby?" he asked.

I smiled. "Oh, it was pretty fun for a kid. My great-aunt knew everyone who lived here and she set up playdates and swim dates and enrolled me in camps and the summer reading program at the library. She worked really hard to make sure I was meeting kids and keeping busy."

Grayson had a way of listening to you that made you feel there was no one else in the world he'd rather be talking to. He leaned in, his expression interested as he tilted his head to one side. "You speak of your aunt really fondly."

"I miss her," I said. "She gave me this perfect, idyllic childhood once I came here. She didn't spare me the chores, either! We'd weed the garden together, plant vegetables, and I'd help her out with the housework. It was just the two of us but I never felt lonely."

"Plus, you had books, I'm guessing."

I chuckled. "Gobs of them. But you've been in the house."

His eyes twinkled. "Books are in stacks against the walls everywhere."

"I couldn't bear to get rid of hers and then I've added a bunch of mine to the mix, too," I said ruefully. "How about you? What's your house like?" I'd never been inside and I was curious.

Grayson made a face. "Typical bachelor mess. Not as cozy as your place. I can't believe I haven't invited you in, considering all the things we've done together." He snapped his fingers. "Which reminds me. I did want to make a special July Fourth edition of the paper and include a recreation section. Do you think you could go on another hike with me? We could make it a picnic and take pictures."

I knew these hiking trips were strictly friend-zone events, but I always enjoyed them. Grayson was very easy to talk to and I'd always feel myself relax. "Sure, that sounds great. There's another spot Luna was reminding me of that I'd totally forgotten about. It should be a nice hike."

"Perfect," said Grayson, smiling. There were golden flecks in his brown eyes that seemed to glow.

Then we heard an unwelcome, raspy voice. "Good to see you two together. I have something to ask you."

I drew back with a gasp. Zelda Smith was our homeowner association president and was constantly campaigning to get Grayson or me on the board. I knew I didn't have any extra time at all to be doing architectural reviews of homeowners' proposed fences or writing emails upbraiding residents on the grass growing through the cracks in their driveway. I suspected Grayson didn't, either.

I was still frozen, but Grayson said in his easy way, "Zelda! Good to see you. Would you like a glass of wine with us?"

Zelda gave him a disapproving look. "Not right at the moment, thank you. I wanted to mention that we're going to have an upcoming vote on adding street lighting to our neighborhood. We have it in the budget and think some attractive lighting might help deter crime as well as be a nice draw to the community."

"Do we have a crime problem?" I asked, startled. I must have missed that neighborhood update.

Zelda glared at me and took a cigarette from her pants pocket, lighting it with a lighter from her other pocket. "Not right now, but you never know. We have teenagers in our neighborhood now."

"Goodness," said Grayson mildly.

Zelda's eyes narrowed as if she suspected he might be making light of the danger. She shook the lit cigarette at him. "Mark my words, those teenagers will mean trouble. They'll be breaking into cars, walking into unlocked homes. Spray-painting graffiti! We need to keep our eyes on them."

"Will do," I said, resisting the urge to salute.

"And, of course, we could use some fresh insight and leadership on the homeowner association board," continued Zelda, giving us both a hard look.

Grayson's and my smiles froze.

Grayson politely said, "As soon as my schedule opens up, I'll be sure to give you a call."

I had just taken a large gulp of my wine, and it instantly made me start coughing as it went down the wrong lane.

Grayson patted me on the back as I coughed, and Zelda frowned at me. "Drinking isn't all it's cut out to be, is it?" she said smugly. "Lesson learned."

She vanished as quickly as she'd appeared.

Grayson said wryly, "As if smoking is much better than drinking."

I finally stopped coughing and grinned at him. "Right."

Grayson stood up. "Well, I should be heading along before I get any more pitches to join the homeowner association board."

I stood up too. "I'll keep an eye on you until you get home. Just in case there are any errant teens around."

He chuckled and waved as he headed out to the sidewalk. I gathered our glasses and brought them inside.

I made Fitz some supper—a lovely mix of poultry and tuna in a can which he somehow seemed to thoroughly enjoy. For myself, I had an equally-lovely mix of leftovers from the previous two nights. The previous two nights had actually been something I'd whipped up with *other* leftover ingredients from various suppers, so having the remainders together was pretty much the visual equivalent of Fitz's odd poultry and tuna mix.

Then I got cleaned up and found Fitz already waiting for me on the bed, looking pleased with himself. He definitely had memorized my routine . . . but how could he help it when every day was very much like Groundhog Day around here. I picked up my current book, *This Tender Land*, which reminded me quite a bit of a modern *Huckleberry Finn*, and settled into the bed. Fitz immediately curled his furry body against me and gave a mew of contentment.

I fell asleep early which meant I woke up really early, too. It was four-thirty when I finally abandoned my bid for sleep and got up for the day. Fitz barely opened his eyes, giving me a disbelieving look. He quickly decided he'd stay where he was, except to move to the warm spot on the bed where I'd been lying.

Since I was up so early, I figured I might as well be productive about it. Feeling bad about not exercising with Grayson last night, I put on my exercise clothes to go out for a short run. I stretched and then headed outside, locking the door behind me. The sunrise was just a hint in the sky as I headed out with a slow lope.

When I came home, I got cleaned up and dressed and fed Fitz, who'd finally abandoned the bed to stand politely next to his food bowl. I fed him, poured myself a bowl of cereal, and then powered up my laptop and answered emails.

After all this, I looked at the clock and found it was still technically too early to go to work. However . . . the library was my favorite place, especially in the early-morning hours when no one else was there. Fitz liked the quiet there too, although he was definitely more extroverted than me.

I coaxed Fitz into his cat carrier and we piled into the car and headed out. During the short drive to the library I passed other homes with people starting out for walks and jogs, taking their dog out, or grabbing their newspaper as the small town of Whitby came to life.

I pulled into the library parking lot and into a space. I frowned at the sight of Ellie's car in the parking lot. Maybe she'd accidentally left something at the library last night or maybe her car had broken down. I unloaded Fitz, took my keys from my purse, and climbed the stairs to the back door.

I found the door unlocked . . . the door pushed right open. I grumbled to myself and Fitz looked at me curiously from his carrier.

"Sorry, buddy," I said softly. "If Ellie's at home, she somehow managed to forget actually locking the door. Which is supposedly the most important part of 'locking up.'"

That wasn't all, though. The lights were still on inside. I called out for Ellie and didn't get an answer.

I scanned the room and then walked toward the stacks. That's when I stopped. A huge bookshelf had toppled over—on the lifeless body of Ellie Norman.

Chapter Four

After trying to find a non-existent pulse on Ellie's wrist, I called Burton right away, my fingers shaking as I dialed his number. He answered quickly, sounding like he'd recently woken up. "Ann?"

"Burton. I just came into the library and the door was unlocked and the lights were on. Someone must have pushed the bookcase over on top of her." I was fumbling for words, trying to work out what had happened. Those bookshelves wouldn't just fall over by themselves. Someone must have done it.

Burton's voice was sharp. "On Luna?"

"No, no. On our new librarian—Ellie Norman. It's Ellie."

Relief flooded his voice, just for a moment, before sounding grim again. "Got it. Okay, Ann. Get out of there and wait for me in the parking lot."

He didn't have to tell me twice. I grabbed Fitz's carrier and headed right for the parking lot. The shaking in my hands was now extending to the rest of me and my legs felt weak as I hurried back down the stairs.

I walked over to my car and slumped against it, waiting for the sound of the siren I could hear in the distance to get closer. I glanced across the parking lot and spotted my favorite library patron, Linus, and his dog Ivy walking slowly up to me. Linus was usually dressed up just about as much as Wilson, but for walking Ivy he had on jeans and a golf shirt. He called out, "Everything okay, Ann?"

I shook my head and he walked over.

"Getting a walk in before heading to the library?" I asked, trying to sound light but my voice shook. Linus was a widower who'd fallen into a routine of spending his days at the library, reading in a particular pattern of newspapers, periodicals, fiction, and non-fiction.

He frowned at the shakiness in my voice and said, "That's right." He looked toward the library, which I was clearly not trying to enter, and turned as the sound of the police siren got closer. "What's going on?"

"Our new librarian? Ellie? There's been—I don't know, some sort of accident or something." As I said them, the words felt wrong to me. There was just no way that huge bookshelf toppled on its own. I reached down and rubbed Ivy, whose sweet face was looking up at me with concern.

"And she's not all right?"

"I'm afraid not," I said, a catch in my voice. Ivy reached over and nuzzled me and I rubbed her soft fur some more.

Linus nodded solemnly. "I'm sorry about that."

We both looked quietly at the library until Burton came speeding into the parking lot.

"I'd better let you speak with the police chief," said Linus quietly, clicking his tongue at Ivy who quickly trotted toward the direction of his home.

Burton strode over to me. "Inside?" he asked.

I nodded. "In the fiction stacks." I hesitated. "The door wasn't locked. It couldn't have been an accident, Burton, not with those sturdy bookshelves. I hate to think the killer is still in there, but be careful."

Burton bobbed his head in acknowledgment and headed to the library, hand on the weapon on his hip while I waited restlessly on the sidewalk. I moved Fitz into the shade again as a sunbeam relentlessly sought out his carrier and crouched down to put my fingers through the bars of the carrier. He gently rubbed his face on them. I noticed an expensive sedan had pulled into the parking lot and I frowned. It was too early for patrons to be here and it wasn't Wilson, who was the only other staff member who ever came in this early.

After what seemed like a very long time, Burton came out, treading heavily as he walked toward me. He rubbed his face with his hand and sighed. "What can you tell me about what happened?"

"Not a lot. Ellie traded shifts with me yesterday and locked up instead of opening. I got the impression she was delaying going back home because she and her sister were having a spat."

Burton raised his bushy eyebrows. "A spat?"

"I don't think it was anything serious. Pris, Ellie's sister, is living with Ellie right now because she's going through a divorce. I think they must just be getting on each other's nerves."

Burton nodded grimly. "So, they argued. Ellie decided she'd rather hang out at the library instead of heading home early. And then you were to open up this morning?"

"That's right." I took a deep breath. "I drove up and saw her car was here, which was odd. Then I went up the stairs and noticed the door was unlocked. Ellie should at least have locked the door to the public, even if she'd decided to arrive early for some reason."

Burton gave me a wry look. "That's when you should have called me."

"I know that now, but at the time, I figured maybe Ellie had just forgotten to lock the door."

"Was she like that? Sort of flighty?" asked Burton.

I shook my head. "Not at all, actually. But I was willing to ascribe forgetfulness to her because she does . . . did . . . get on my nerves a lot. Anyway, I saw the lights were on, too, and then I really did get alarmed. I mean, forgetting both things was a lot weirder. That's when I saw Ellie under the bookcase." I paused. "I did feel for a pulse, but I didn't move her or do anything else."

Burton said, "I don't really know Ellie because she's so new. You said she got on your nerves sometimes. Was it just you, or did others feel the same?"

"Well, I know Luna felt the same because we even talked about it yesterday. It's nothing major—just sort of petty work issues. You know the kind—she'd leave early for lunch or take too *long* at lunch. She was nosy and seemed to get into everybody's business."

"How was she nosy?" asked Burton.

I shrugged. "She always seemed to be lurking in the stacks, listening in on people's conversations. A couple of times, I noticed Ellie listening in on the staff's phone calls."

Burton nodded thoughtfully. "That could have made somebody upset, listening in on the wrong person." He glanced across the parking lot at the expensive sedan that was still idling. "Who's that?"

I followed his gaze to the car in the parking lot and tried to make out the person behind the wheel. "You know, I think that's the guy Ellie has been having lunches with."

Burton's bushy eyebrows flew up. "Really? Well, I definitely want to speak to him, then. Are you sure about that?"

"Pretty sure. It's the same car, anyway. Luna has remarked on it, too."

"Let's have a little chat with him before the state police shows up with the forensics team," said Burton, heading in the direction of the sedan.

The man in the expensive car had dark, wavy hair and the kind of tan that looked as if he might have acquired it on the golf course. He frowned a little when he saw the police chief and me walking toward him and reluctantly put his window down.

"Hi, officer," he said formally.

Burton said, "Good morning, sir. I'm the police chief, Burton Edison. Just wondering how you came to be at the library this early in the morning." He gestured toward me and said, "It's even early for the librarian to be here, much less a patron."

The man cleared his throat. "Well, I actually saw your lights and heard the siren and thought I'd see what had happened at the library."

Burton quirked a brow as if to indicate that was an odd thing to do.

The man took a deep breath and continued, "I knew the library wasn't open yet, so I was curious as to what emergency might be happening there so early. That's all."

"Is it?" drawled Burton.

Burton had an effective way of drawing out people that I had seen him use before. He just got very quiet and didn't say a word. The person would get more and more uncomfortable as the silence dragged on and would finally fill it. This man did, too.

He cleared his throat again. "I'm Ted Griffith, by the way. You're right—I know one of the librarians here. Her name is Ellie and I thought I remembered she was opening up the library today."

The last part was directed at me, but I wasn't sure how much Burton wanted to disclose, so I glanced over at him.

Burton said, "Well, that's very interesting. You must be good friends with her, Mr. Griffith, if you're that familiar with her work schedule."

Now Ted looked even more uncomfortable than he had before. "Not really. I've been helping to teach her Spanish. She was interested in learning and I'm fairly fluent."

"That's very educational-sounding," said Burton levelly. He was quiet for a moment as if trying to decide something. Then he said, "I'm sorry to have to tell you this, but your instincts were right. Ellie is deceased."

Ted's face turned white and I realized it was a good thing he was sitting down. "What happened to her?"

"We're trying to figure that out," said Burton. His voice was a little gentler. "I'm sorry. It sounds like you cared about her."

Ted said, "As a friend. Of course I did. I was in the library one day and she struck up a conversation with me. She was very outgoing. I was reading a book in Spanish and she said she'd always wanted to learn Spanish but had taken French in school. So I started up some casual classes over lunch to help teach her the language."

"Where were you last night?" asked Burton, abruptly changing topics.

Ted's face grew even paler than it was. "What?"

"It's standard procedure," said Burton without much inflection in his voice.

Ted stuttered, "Well, I was sleeping, of course."

"Earlier than that. Say around nine o'clock."

Ted said slowly, "At home with my wife. Probably reading that Spanish literature book."

Burton took out a small notebook from his pocket and jotted down a couple of notes. He looked up at Ted again. "If it turns out to be foul play, do you have any idea who might be connected? Has Ellie talked about any problems she's had with anyone? Any arguments?"

Ted considered this for a few moments. "Well, we didn't spend much time talking about personal things. But I think she mentioned a bit of conflict with her sister. Pris is her name, I think. It sounded just like everyday irritation from having somebody move in with you." He glanced longingly at the road. "I should be getting along. I have to go to work."

Burton said, "Absolutely, sir. I wouldn't want to hold you up. I just need to have your contact information."

Ted hurriedly provided it to him and drove away.

Burton looked over at me and said, "Seems to be more to that story than Spanish lessons."

"I didn't know Ellie really well, but I'd never heard her mention foreign language lessons to me. Nor a deep desire to learn Spanish." I hesitated. "Luna thought they were having a relationship. We saw Ted's wife, Sunny, come into the library yesterday and there seemed to be some tension there."

"His wife approached Ellie?" asked Burton.

"No. Actually, Ellie approached Sunny."

Burton snorted. "Well, she had guts."

"Or something. Sunny is on the board of trustees for the library and was there to speak with Wilson." I paused. "Or, at least, that's the way it seemed." I glanced at my watch. "Oh gosh. I really need to call Wilson."

Burton bobbed his head toward an approaching vehicle. "No need. Looks like your director is coming right now."

The state police also seemed to be coming up and Burton walked off to speak with them.

Wilson pulled his car up alongside me and hopped out, looking anxious. "Ann, what's going on?"

I took a deep breath and filled him in. Wilson's face grew even more concerned as I continued. We stared in solemn silence at the library when I finished.

Wilson said slowly, "There's no way those shelves fell by themselves."

"No," I agreed. "They were sturdy."

"Someone did this. To Ellie."

I nodded silently. We watched as the state police and Burton strung up police tape around the library.

Wilson asked, "Could you go to the office supply store and pick up materials to make a sign to indicate the library is closed today? I'll call Luna and the other staff members and ask Luna to post on social media to let everyone know we're temporarily closed."

I nodded again and watched as Burton approached us. He said to Wilson, "I'm going to need Ellie's address and other information so I can notify her sister."

"Of course. I can pull that up on my laptop here." Wilson turned to me and said, "Actually, that reminds me, Ann. Can you make some arrangements for the library to bring food for Ellie's sister on behalf of the library for tomorrow?"

I told him I would and left while he spoke to Burton. I came back half an hour later with two poster board signs, which I put on both library doors. I saw Luna drive up and walked over to her car.

Her eyes were huge. "Ann, what happened?"

I gave her a quick rundown and Luna frowned. "The shelf came down on her? What?"

"I know. I didn't think that was a very likely scenario, either."

Luna gave a low whistle. "So you're thinking somebody did that intentionally. That somebody pushed a huge shelving unit on top of Ellie on purpose."

"I can't see any other way it would have happened. She wouldn't have pulled it down on herself and it wouldn't have just spontaneously fallen like that. It's not as if Wilson would have allowed anything unsafe to be in the library. It would be a liability otherwise."

We were quiet for a few moments before Luna said slowly, "You know, I didn't really *like* Ellie, but I never wanted something like this to happen. I simply wanted her to take her lunch breaks when she was supposed to and maybe stop being so nosy." She stopped suddenly and looked at me. "You don't think her nosiness had something to do with this?"

"I don't know. But it might have."

Burton saw I was speaking with Luna and waved to her. She smiled and waved back. "He's always so friendly, isn't he?" she asked.

Friendlier to Luna than he was to me, I thought with a smile. "He sure is. He's a nice guy," I said pointedly.

Luna didn't respond, instead, she glanced across the parking lot. "Look, it's Linus. He'll be disappointed the library is closed today."

I furrowed my eyebrows. "Actually, he was by earlier, so he knows it's going to be closed. He must be here for another reason."

Linus now wore his usual suit and came up to Luna and me with a serious expression on his face, sans Ivy this time.

"I'm very sorry about your colleague," he said in his quiet, earnest voice. He glanced toward Burton, who was speaking with a state policeman. He hesitated. "There was just something I thought might possibly be important and I thought I should mention it to the police chief. I hope I'm not wasting his time or implicating someone who's completely innocent."

Luna's eyes were wide. "What did you see?"

"Well, I was sitting in my car a few days earlier and just gathering my library books together. I'd decided to drive since it

looked like it might rain later—you know I usually walk over."
Linus looked a little anxious.

I smiled encouragingly. "And something happened in the parking lot?"

He nodded. "The new librarian—Ellie, I believe you said her name was—she was arguing with another woman nearby. I wasn't trying to listen in, but it was very hard not to overhear them. In fact, hearing them so clearly reminded me that I needed to put one of my car windows up."

"What were they saying?" asked Luna.

Linus winced as if reluctant to say. "It sounded as if Ellie was trying to blackmail the other woman. I couldn't tell for *sure*, of course, but she was saying something like she intended on releasing information if the woman didn't pay her. That she'd be sorry."

"Did you recognize the other woman?" I asked.

Linus nodded again. "That is, I recognized her, but don't know her. She wears her hair in a ponytail, looks very young, and I see her from time to time working in that coffee shop on the square."

Luna put a hand to her mouth. "Tara Fuller!"

Linus quickly interjected, "Like I mentioned, I don't know exactly what I overheard, and I might have misinterpreted it. I certainly don't want to get anyone into any trouble when they had nothing to do with this business. But when I was home with Ivy, I kept thinking I should let the police know about it, just in case."

"You did the right thing," I said to reassure the older man.

"Absolutely," said Luna with a weak smile.

Linus cleared his throat. "Well, it looks as if Burton is free now, so I'll go speak with him. Thanks for lending an ear, and sorry again about Ellie."

Luna looked at me urgently. "Let's go to the coffee shop. I want to talk to Tara."

Chapter Five

I sighed. "Luna, I don't think it's a good idea to go interrogate Tara."

"I'm not going to *interrogate* her. I just want to find out what Ellie was trying to blackmail her over."

I stared at Luna. This all sounded very much like an interrogation.

Luna said, "I've just become friends with Tara and I think trying to make sure she's okay is a friendly thing to do, that's all. Besides, this is the perfect time for us to go since we don't have any work today. Then, after this, maybe I can reschedule my mom's doctor's visit to this afternoon so I won't have to take that afternoon off next week."

I could tell she was already mentally ticking off boxes of things to do. I said, "The only thing is that I have Fitz with me."

We glanced down at the carrier and Fitz blinked up at us in his laid-back way. He seemed perfectly content in his carrier during all of this. Wilson had kept an eye on him for me when I'd gone to the store for the supplies for the sign.

Luna said, "Run him home and get him settled. I'll follow you and then drive you to the coffee shop. Remember your goal—to get out of the house more."

I wasn't sure if this was my goal or Luna's goal. But I nodded. I could tell when Luna was totally determined.

A few minutes later, I'd gotten Fitz settled into a bright sunbeam on my kitchen floor. He drowsily curled up into a ball with his fluffy tail over his nose and quickly fell asleep. I joined Luna in her car, and we headed out.

The coffee shop was on the same square the library was situated on. It was a beautiful old square, with the town hall in the middle and old oaks scattered throughout. The coffee shop was called "Keep Grounded." I had to admit I felt my spirits lift a little when I walked in, and it wasn't just because I was about to get caffeine. The shop was a cheerful place with brick walls, light streaming through the many windows, inviting bookshelves, and brightly painted wooden chairs and tables.

Tara was just as Linus had described her, and was wiping down an already spotless table when we came in. She was probably in her late twenties and had her dark hair up in a jaunty ponytail. She wore an apron with "Keep Grounded" and their coffee cup logo on it. She gave them both a warm grin and said, "Luna! Hey girl, how are you?"

Luna hugged her back fiercely and blurted out, "Tara, was Ellie blackmailing you?"

I sighed, glad we were the only customers in the shop. I hadn't even been formally introduced to Tara and Luna was already trying to strongarm her secrets out of her. I cleared my throat and Luna added absently, "Oh, and this is Ann. She works with me."

Tara was at a total loss for words and turned a little pale.

Luna finally noticed Tara's expression and gave her another hug. "Sorry! I'm sorry. I'm just so worried about you."

Tara looked desperate to get her bearings before being dragged into a conversation she didn't want to have. She hesitantly asked us if she could get us some coffees and looked relieved as she went through the familiar motions of making them. Then she gave me a bright smile as she gestured to my e-reader.

"What are you reading? I've haven't read anything for a while and I really miss it."

I smiled back at her. "*House of Mirth*."

Luna snorted. "A little light reading."

I said, "It's a favorite of mine, so I was re-reading it. But I'd be happy to give you a few suggestions, if you can tell me genres you enjoy."

We spent the next few minutes chatting about books and I jotted down some ideas for titles on a napkin and handed it to Tara.

Then Tara became solemn. "How did you hear about the blackmail?" she finally asked in a small voice.

Luna threw up her hands. "Hearsay. You know how it is in a small town. So it's true then?"

Tara sighed. "Gotta love small towns, right? Yes, it's true. Sort of."

"Sort of?" pressed Luna, brow wrinkling in concern.

"Yes. I used to be friends with Ellie, before she started blackmailing me, of course." Tara gave a short laugh. "She was fun, and I needed someone to do things with."

Luna said, "*We're* going to do fun things, Tara. I can promise no blackmail will be involved."

"I appreciate that," said Tara, eyes finally getting a little twinkle back in them. "Anyway, I was working at my hospital job before here—you remember I told you about it, Luna?"

"Right. You were working in the pharmacy at the regional hospital."

Whitby was too small to qualify for its own hospital, but fortunately there was a large regional hospital that served the county.

"Exactly." Tara absently laid down the cleaning cloth she was still clutching in her hand. "I'm not proud of this, but I used to be addicted to prescription painkillers." A flush rose from her neck, staining her cheeks.

Luna gave her another quick hug. "You poor thing."

"They really took over my life. I had no idea what I was in for. I'd been in a car accident a couple of years ago and the doctor prescribed them for the back pain I was having. It was the kind of pain that was just always around—I couldn't shake it. I guess I must have an addictive personality though, because I ended up getting hooked."

"And Ellie somehow found out about it?" I asked.

Tara nodded. "I was desperate," she said in a soft voice. "I was out of drugs and having withdrawal side effects. Plus, I was low-energy and had lost weight. I looked really awful."

Looking at Tara now, it was hard to imagine. She was the picture of health. Tara was clearly free from the grasp of addiction now.

I said, "Ellie always seemed really perceptive." And, I thought, very nosy.

"Exactly. She noticed and asked me right away what was wrong. When I hesitated, she asked if I was 'on something.' She said my eyes were really bloodshot. As soon as she asked me, I couldn't help but spill everything. I was so relieved to finally tell somebody and ask for help."

Luna said, "So you asked Ellie to help find you a way to stop using the prescription drugs?"

Tara snorted. "You're sweet, Luna. I can tell you've never been an addict. No, I'm afraid I *didn't* ask for her help to stop using. Instead, I asked Ellie for money."

What did Ellie say?" I asked curiously.

"Oh, she seemed worried about me, and super-supportive," said Tara bitterly. "But I didn't think about one thing until later."

"What's that?" asked Luna.

"The fact she was pumping me for information. I thought she was just being a good friend and being an ear for me . . . letting me spill out all my troubles. But she was really just gathering all my secrets and the fact I worked at a sensitive job: with pharmaceuticals at the hospital. Once she got everything she needed, she started asking *me* for money."

I said quietly, "But you weren't really in a position to pay."

"Of course not. I laughed in her face when she asked me. *I* was the one originally asking *her* for money."

"So what did you do?" asked Luna.

"What *could* I do? I didn't have anything to pay her with. I couldn't even afford my own habit. That's when the hospital laid me off, too—nothing to do with my drug use. I got the job here, cleaned myself up, and tried to get my life back on track."

"Did Ellie give up with the blackmail demands?" I asked. My mind returned to Linus and the fact he'd just overheard Ellie and Tara only a few days earlier.

"Nope. I don't think 'giving up' is a phrase Ellie is familiar with. She's still trying to shake me down. Y'all work with her every day, so watch your backs. Keep your secrets to yourselves."

Luna and I looked at each other as we realized we hadn't given Tara the news yet.

"Tara, that's why we're here. Ellie is dead," said Luna.

A mix of emotions passed over Tara's features. I saw relief, which I expected and understood, but also a glimpse of surprise and then, finally, concern.

"What do you mean? Was she in a car accident or something?"

Luna shook her head. "We think someone murdered her."

Now Tara backed away from us and sank abruptly into a chair. "No," she said quietly.

"But think about it," said Luna, walking toward her. "Now you're *free*. She won't be trying to force you to pay her anymore. You won't have to avoid her or worry about it."

Tara shook her head. "But look who's the prime suspect, Luna."

I said, "Tara, if Ellie was blackmailing you, there are probably others, too. Ellie was very good at lurking around, I noticed."

Luna nodded solemnly. "I just thought she was super-nosy. So there are probably other people who wanted Ellie out of the way, too. Other suspects. Besides, don't you have an alibi for Ellie's death?"

"For when?" asked Tara. She brightened. "I've been here at the coffee shop all morning. I opened up today."

I said, "What about last night?"

"Last night?"

I said, "We don't really know when Ellie's death happened."

Tara looked relieved. "I was working a late shift last night, too. I've been trying to get as many hours in as possible lately since my rent was based on my income from when I worked at the hospital."

"Good," said Luna stoutly. "Well, you shouldn't have anything to worry about then, should you?"

Tara looked thoughtful. "You know, Ann, when you said Ellie might be blackmailing other people too? I've just remembered something. She *did* know a secret about one guy because she mentioned it to me when we were still 'friends.' Frank Morrison."

I raised my eyebrows. "The guy who does IT work for the library?"

"Right. He also runs by here daily for coffee, and the owner sometimes uses him to help with our internet connection. Anyway, Ellie was friends with Frank's wife, Judith."

"*Real* friends or potential blackmail victim?" asked Luna.

"Real friends. Ellie noticed a lot of bruises on Judith's arms and neck and asked her about them. Ellie always did a good job of seeming concerned. Judith broke down and told her Frank was abusive."

"That's awful," I said soberly. I didn't fancy having Frank do work for the library if that was the kind of person he was. It was hearsay, but I made a mental note to speak to Wilson about it and run it by him.

Tara nodded. "I know. Ellie said Judith admitted she was drinking too much as a sort of coping mechanism. Then she died a couple of weeks later."

"A suspicious death?" asked Luna, eyes narrowing.

"That's what Ellie was saying. Judith apparently fell down the stairs and broke her neck. But maybe Frank pushed her. I bet Ellie was blackmailing Frank. She probably told him she'd tell the cops if he didn't pay up."

"The police weren't already investigating her death?" I asked.

"Apparently, they thought it was an accident," said Tara with a shrug. "According to a neighbor who's a regular here, Judith had a lot of alcohol in her blood."

"Well, I guess so if she was trying to deal with abuse!" said Luna indignantly.

The door to the coffee shop opened and a group of moms with toddlers came in. The toddlers went straight over to a low-hanging blackboard and started scribbling with the chalk there.

"We'd better let you run," I said.

Tara gave us both a smile and a wave. "See you later!"

Luna and I headed out toward Luna's car and a voice behind me said, "Ann Beckett?"

I turned around to see a guy in his early thirties with curly blond hair, the bluest of blue eyes, and an impish smile on his face. "Connor Rogers?" I asked with a laugh.

Luna looked at both of us and quirked an eyebrow.

"Well, look at you all grown up," Connor laughed, giving me an enthusiastic hug before drawing back to look at me again. "Wow, it's good to see you."

"You, too." I gave him a bemused smile, still sort of stunned by seeing an unexpected vision from my past.

"Perhaps an introduction is in order?" drawled Luna.

I cleared my throat and gave another little laugh. "Absolutely. Luna, this is Connor. Connor, Luna. Connor and I used to go to school together back in the day."

"Which is possibly the driest introduction in the world, although technically true," said Connor, blue eyes twinkling mischievously. "What Ann didn't say is that we used to date on and off through high school."

"High school was actually *fun* then?" asked Luna with a wide grin. "I really know someone who *enjoyed* their high school experience?"

I said, "*Enjoy* might be a stretch, but we did have fun. Football games on Friday nights, going to the movies, walking the trails. So are you back in town now, Connor?"

"Sure am. I was in Charlotte, but decided to move back to Whitby to be closer to my folks. I took a job over at the regional hospital."

I said, "Oh, what do you do over there?"

"I'm in emergency medicine. A doctor," said Connor with a shrug. He smiled at me again. "It's really good to see you again,

Ann. How about supper tonight?" He paused. "And bring your husband, of course."

"No husband," I said, flushing a little.

"Great!" Connor's face brightened and I could see the two dimples I remembered from high school.

I hesitated. "The only thing is there's something I have to do for work."

Luna looked at me as if I were insane. "Work? We just got the day off, Ann."

"What work do you do?" Connor asked.

"I'm a librarian," I said, flushing again. It somehow didn't sound quite as flashy as emergency room physician.

"I can *totally* see you doing that," said Connor. "You always had your nose in a book and I was so intimidated because I'd be playing video games or something stupid and you'd have just finished some impossible James Joyce novel in a day."

I snorted. "Definitely not in a day. And almost certainly not Joyce."

Luna said, "Excuse me, Ann, but what library work are you referring to? Because I find it hard to believe Wilson tasked you with something under the circumstances. If he did, then I need to help you out with it because that's totally unfair."

"Oh, he asked for us to arrange to bring food to Pris on behalf of the library," I said.

Luna said, "I'll go with you to handle it. But seriously, that's only going to take a few minutes and, by definition, the food probably needs to get to Pris *before* dinnertime so she doesn't go through the bother of preparing something herself."

I turned to Connor and said, "Supper would be amazing, then, thanks."

"Great! Where's a good place to go? I haven't been here for ages and I'm sure there are lots more restaurants."

Luna and I looked at each other and chuckled. "Actually, there are probably the same options we had when we were in high school."

"So, Quittin' Time it is?" asked Connor with a grin.

There was another option, but it was sort of a special occasion place and I didn't want to give him the wrong impression. Quittin' Time, with its fried food and meat and three veggie plates, was a lot more casual. "Perfect. How about if we meet at 6:30?"

"It's a date. See you then!" and Connor, whistling to himself, walked into the coffee shop.

Chapter Six

"It's a date, hmm?" asked Luna in a teasing voice as we got into her car. "Goodbye Grayson, hello Connor!"

I laughed and shook my head. "I don't think that's what Connor meant, Luna. You're taking him very literally. We're just two old friends catching up, that's all."

Luna waggled her eyebrows at me. "Two old friends who used to be an item. Well, Grayson is missing out, but that's what happens when somebody takes too long to develop a relationship, right? What were you and Connor like together when you were dating?"

"That was like forever ago!"

Luna rolled her eyes as she drove down the tree-lined street to my house. "Right. Yeah, you're *so old* now. Come on, that was just like fifteen years ago. You must have gotten some sort of impression from your time together."

I thought back to high school, which was a kind of mesh of memories—math classes I dreaded, English classes I loved, evenings of hanging out with friends . . . and Connor. "He was fun. We had a good time together. He was always my date to stuff like Homecoming or the prom or when friends had get-togethers."

"What made the two of you break up?" asked Luna curiously.

"Oh, I don't know. Probably it had something to do with the fact we were seventeen or eighteen years old and weren't exactly mature. We didn't have the kind of relationship where we wanted to go to the same college or anything. Neither of us wanted to be tied down when we went off to school—we wanted to be free to meet new people."

Luna said with a smirk, "Well he certainly seemed very interested in continuing where the two of you left off."

"No way. I really think he's just wanting to catch up and talk about the old days. I mean, he even asked if I wanted to bring my husband along. Maybe I'll show up tonight and he'll have his wife there with him."

Luna snorted. "Right. Did you see how delighted he looked when you said you weren't married? He looked like it was his birthday and Christmas all rolled into one. I don't think there's a wife anywhere on the scene. Do you realize how hard it is to find a good guy to date here in Whitby? I feel like I'm getting nowhere fast."

Once again, I found myself biting my tongue. If Luna just opened her eyes to the possibilities around her, she'd realize Burton was carrying a torch for her. More than a torch—more like a flaming inferno. But I just grunted in response, thinking Luna really did need to figure it out for herself.

"Plus, he's a *doctor*. That means he's smart and he's a hard worker. It's very *hard* to find a smart, hardworking single guy here," stressed Luna.

I nodded, mainly to keep Luna from continuing to sing this refrain. "Got it. You're right. I didn't say no to supper tonight, remember? I'm meeting up with him later and we'll see how it goes. But I know from experience not to expect too much." I was really ready to change the subject at this point. "Now, what should we do about Pris?"

"Pris?" Luna, deep in her thoughts about my nonexistent love life, sounded as if she'd never heard the name before.

"Ellie's sister. We need to bring her supper in a few hours and you've got a doctor's appointment. I don't have a lot of stuff in my fridge." My refrigerator, never really bursting with food, was especially barren right now.

Luna frowned. "Maybe today isn't the best day to cook. Maybe we should just pick something up somewhere and put a nice note with it."

"That might be the better idea. Unfortunately, I don't really know anything about what Pris likes to eat. Is her daughter with her now? I know she goes back and forth between Pris and her dad."

Luna pulled into my street and then my driveway and took out her phone. "There's only one way to handle this. We should call her."

I shifted uncomfortably in my seat. "Should we? She just found out about her sister's death a little while ago."

"There's really no other way to figure out how many mouths we're feeding, if there are food allergies, or when might be a good time to drop by the food," said Luna with a shrug. "I'll be tactful."

Luna could sometimes be very direct, so I'll admit I treated that statement with a bit of skepticism. But the ensuing phone call made me realize Luna could indeed be tactful and very sympathetic. When Luna hung up with Pris, she had all the pertinent information and had also passed along our condolences in a very kind manner.

"Okay," she said. "We're in business. Pris is by herself right now—her ex has her daughter right now. She is happy to eat anything apparently, has no food allergies, and seemed very grateful for the meal. She said five-thirty would work out great."

"Perfect," I said with relief. We made plans to pick up a fried chicken dinner with all the fixings from a local spot and then Luna left for home.

As I walked up the front walk, I saw the front curtains rustle and Fitz peered out curiously at me before blinking and giving me a contented look. I opened the door and he leapt off the end table to greet me, wrapping his tail around my legs and purring loudly.

"Hey there, sweetie," I crooned to him. "Did you miss me? I guess you must have gotten some good naptime in, right?"

He certainly did seem alert and not at all sleepy. I pulled out his favorite toy; a fishing pole that had a fuzzy chicken attached to the end of it. I wasn't sure what the manufacturer had been thinking of when they'd put the odd toy together, but Fitz loved it and scampered after the chicken as I made it bounce around the room with the fishing line.

After exercising Fitz, I realized I needed to exercise myself, too. I was about to head to the park for a fast walk when I hesitated. Maybe I should reach out to Grayson. He had a pretty flexible schedule as the newspaper editor, and a lot of his features were prepared in advance, from what I remembered. I took a deep breath and grabbed my phone before I could change my mind.

"*The Whitby Times*," Grayson answered on the other end.

"Um, hi," I said, and was instantly irritated at how vapid I frequently sounded when speaking with Grayson. "Due to unexpected circumstances, I have the day off. Obviously, I know you're still working, but I wondered if you'd like to take that hike and have that picnic today instead of later on."

"That would ordinarily be great, but right now I've got to write a story about your unexpected circumstances," said Grayson.

Right. I somehow didn't think about the fact that a murder in the library would change the trajectory of Grayson's day about as much as it did mine—but with *more* work on his end.

"Got it. That makes total sense."

Grayson said, "Maybe tomorrow? Are you free then?"

"Actually, I'm going to be working tomorrow and the next day. You know what, maybe I should just send you my work schedule so we can figure out when to make it work."

"That sounds good," he said. "Sorry about today." But he already sounded a little distracted, as if his head were back in the article he was writing.

I hung up and looked at Fitz. "Okay, so I *am* going to the park, then."

Fitz rolled on his back and gave me a lazy look as if suggesting I'd be much happier if I just curled up with him and took a nice nap on the sofa. Maybe he was right, but if I did that, I definitely wouldn't feel like squeezing some exercise and a shower in before Luna and I went to Pris's house. Then I remembered I had an unexpected dinner with Connor to ready myself for, and I probably should think about what I was going to wear. With this on my mind, I changed into workout clothes and headed to the park.

I had a slow jog, taking in the beauty of the park as I jogged around the small lake on one of the paths. The mountains were in the background, there were birds of different varieties at the feeders town volunteers had put out, and the trees provided shade from the heat as I went. There were a good number of moms with young children out at the playground not far from the trail and several folks walking their dogs. I kept an eye out for Linus, thinking maybe he'd take Ivy back out again since the library was closed, but I didn't see him.

After the jog, I walked for a while to get my heart rate down, then headed back home to get showered and ready for the rest of the day. I fed Fitz, then Luna texted me to say she was waiting outside so I hurried out to join her.

"You're looking rather pleased with yourself," said Luna with a wink. "Is that because you have a date later?"

"More than that," I said.

Luna's eyes widened. "What? Do you have *two* dates?"

"No, no," I said with a laugh. "Forget the dating. I mean I actually motivated myself to go exercise this afternoon. I'm one of those people who absolutely hates exercising but feels incredibly smug after it's all done."

Luna looked gloomy. "Ah. You should have called me up. That's exactly what I keep telling myself *I'm* going to be doing when I have free time. Instead, I end up goofing off."

"I thought you were taking your mom to the doctor this afternoon."

"Oh, I did. It just happened to be the quickest doctor appointment in the history of the world. Usually we have to sit in the waiting room for thirty minutes and then we end up waiting in the exam room for another twenty. Somehow, this time it was all going like a well-oiled machine. Anyway, I need to be exercising more. Maybe I'll start taking my bike to work again."

Ellie's house was a two-story white house with black shutters and a wrap-around porch. She'd apparently had something of a green thumb because the yard was vibrant with perennials and flowering bushes. I remembered the house as it had been before she'd moved in and its yard had been remarkable only in its distinctly blah look. Clearly, she'd planned and executed it. It meant she and I had had *something* in common and I wondered if I'd tried a little harder if she and I would have gotten along better. Then I thought about the blackmailing and figured we wouldn't have.

Pris answered the door looking pale and shaken. When she saw Luna and me, she broke into a tight smile.

"This is so sweet of you two," she said. Her voice sounded crackly, like she'd been crying.

"We don't want to make you visit," I said quickly. "We just wanted to tell you how sorry we are. From the entire library."

Pris smiled again, this time a slightly more natural one. She hesitated. "Do you have time? Not long, I mean. Just a few minutes? I feel like I want to talk this out with somebody and Ellie was all I had here." Her voice broke at the end and she pulled a tissue out of her pocket to swab at her face.

"Of course we do," said Luna warmly and I nodded in agreement.

Pris stepped aside, opening the door wide and Luna and I followed her in.

The house was very dim inside with no curtains opened nor many lights on. I wondered if Pris had still been sleeping when Burton came over to speak with her. Luna noticed it too. "Want me to open the curtains? Turn some lights on?"

Pris nodded, looking around at the dimness as if just noticing it for the first time as Luna and I brought back some light into the living room. Now that I could look around a little, I could see Ellie's decorating skills at work in the house. There were some old chairs that looked like they'd been reupholstered in floral fabrics. There were pops of color everywhere with bright cushions scattered on the sofa and chairs.

Pris seemed lost in her own thoughts again and Luna and I glanced at each other before finding places to sit down. We waited, saying nothing, until Pris was ready to speak. Finally, she took a deep breath and said, "I just can't believe she's gone."

I said, "It must have been a terrible shock when you were told this morning."

"I know *we* were shocked," said Luna, looking at me.

Pris said, "I was sleeping in when there was a knock on the door. I stopped by Ellie's room to see if she knew who might be at the door. But she wasn't there." She gave a shiver and I felt a corresponding chill up my spine. It must have been awful for her to start putting two and two together when she'd seen Burton at her door.

"I thought it might be Ellie at the door. Like she'd gone out for breakfast or something and had forgotten her key. But it didn't make any sense. Ellie had closed up the library last night so why would she be up early this morning? Then I went to the door and looked out and saw the police chief there." She exhaled a shaky breath. "He must have had to tell me three or four times what had happened because it just wasn't sinking in."

Luna gave her a sympathetic look. "Of course it wasn't. You'd never expect anything to happen to Ellie. Why would you? She was young and strong."

Pris nodded. "Burton ended up making me a strong cup of coffee because I thought I was going to keel over. I kept shivering, too. He was really kind."

I found myself glancing over at Luna, hoping she was taking in the fact that Burton had been so nice to Pris. That he was a thoughtful, kind man who was very dateable material. Luna, as usual, seemed oblivious.

"We're so lucky to have him as the police chief," agreed Luna. "He's been great about working with the youth in Whitby, too."

Pris nodded, looking troubled. "I know this is usually a safe place to live, otherwise I wouldn't be trying to move my daughter here." She glanced at us. "I know I've mentioned this a little bit before when I've seen you in the library because it sort of consumes my life. Right now, I have joint custody, but my ex is a lawyer and I'm worried he's going to pull some sort of stunt and I'll end up not being able to see my little girl. I've been just sick over it."

Luna drew her brows together. "Of course you have been! What a rotten thing for him to try and do."

"And now this happened." Pris put her head in her hands and rubbed her eyes with the base of her palms. "I feel so awful about it. Ellie and I were really bumping heads yesterday—you saw some of that, Ann."

I shrugged, feeling uncomfortable about verifying a disagreement that Pris clearly felt guilty over. "All families have tiffs."

"It's true. I think it was all the stress I've been under that was making me really irritable. Ellie was awesome to let me move in and I tried to be the perfect houseguest at first. I made supper most nights, especially since Ellie has been working in the evenings. I've helped her in the yard, even if I suspected she really didn't want me to." Pris gave us a rueful grin.

"I could tell, coming in, that Ellie must really have loved working outside," I said.

Pris nodded, her eyes welling up a little until she furiously blinked the tears back down again. "She did. It must have been stress relief for her, which is something I didn't totally understand. But boy, after I pulled a couple of 'weeds' that ended up being perennials, she let me know about it. Anyway, I did try to pull my own weight around here, but the stress was hard for me to overcome. I mean, I was already a total basket-case because of the upcoming divorce and getting used to being away from my ex and my daughter."

"Which must have been really traumatic," said Luna, giving her a sympathetic look.

"It's been hard." Pris's voice caught a little and she cleared her throat before continuing. "Then I've been trying to find a job, but I haven't worked in years because my husband and I were trying to have a baby and I had all these doctor appointments. Then, when Melissa was born, I was a full-time mom. So I really feel like I'm not qualified to do much of anything, especially since my self-esteem is at rock bottom."

Luna said, "We'll keep an ear out, won't we, Ann?"

I nodded. "We have an online jobs board that's hosted on the library website, too. That might help you."

She gave us a grateful look. "Thanks so much. Ellie didn't mention that." Her lips pressed together tightly, either in annoyance that Ellie didn't mention the job listings or in grief that her sister was gone.

I added quickly, "Ellie was new to the library, of course, and might not have known about it."

Pris nodded absently, but her mind was clearly on other things. "And, of course, Ellie and I were totally different people. Grown people who weren't very much alike. Ellie was used to living alone and doing things her way, and then I came crashing in and changed everything. It's been an adjustment for both of us. I'm not sure Ellie was completely sold on being a librarian for the rest of her life. She said something about starting her own business, but didn't offer any details when I asked about it." She looked at us. "What was Ellie like? I mean, to work with?"

Luna and I glanced at each other. I had no plans on speaking ill of the dead, especially to my coworker's sister. I said carefully, "Ellie was very organized. She was a hard worker."

Luna nodded in fervent agreement.

Pris looked as if she might press us on the matter, but then let it go. Then she said, "Ann, you found her this morning, right?"

I nodded, feeling uncomfortable.

"Burton told me it was a suspicious death," said Pris. "He said she must have died last night."

That was actually more information than we'd had, so it was good to hear it confirmed. "When I walked in this morning, I was worried because the library door wasn't locked and the lights were still on. It does make sense that it happened last night."

Pris's face again creased with guilt and worry. "If I'd only been there. I was irritated with Ellie and wanted to turn in early so I didn't have to see her when she came in after nine. I got ready for bed and then had my earbuds in and watched a movie on my laptop. After that, I turned on my white noise sound machine and fell asleep. I figured Ellie was safely back home."

"You couldn't have known," said Luna stoutly. "If you *had* gone to the library to investigate, who knows what might have happened? Maybe you would have been attacked, yourself."

They were quiet for a moment or two and then Pris said, "I've been trying to think about who might have done this to Ellie. It just seemed so totally far-fetched. But then, the more I started thinking about it, the more I started realizing that maybe

I *could* see where someone might have wanted Ellie out of the way."

Chapter Seven

"Like who?" I asked quietly.

Pris shrugged, shifting in her seat and looking down. "I don't know. I don't really know what I'm talking about, it's just that I can't stop thinking about it and maybe I'm trying to connect the dots in my head. But Ellie was seeing somebody."

"She had a boyfriend?" I asked.

Pris sighed. "Yes, but he was married. I told her that wasn't right. I told her to put herself in the poor wife's shoes, but she just ignored me. She was really hard-headed when she wanted to be."

Luna said, "Do you think he might have had something to do with what happened to Ellie?"

Pris shrugged, looking weary. "Who knows, right? But I figure the police aren't going to know about it unless I say something to them about him. When the cops were here earlier, I was just so shocked at what they were saying that I didn't even think to say anything about it." She made a face. "Anyway, it was something else Ellie and I were arguing over."

"Who was it?" asked Luna.

"Ted Griffith." Pris sighed. "Ellie seemed to think he was going to leave his wife for her. I told her that wasn't usually the way things worked, but she was convinced." She hesitated. "I wondered if maybe Ellie was putting pressure on Ted to leave his wife. Sunny, I think her name is. Okay, I actually *know* she was. She told him that unless he was going to leave his wife, she was going to tell Sunny about their relationship. Then she'd wreck their marriage and he wouldn't have *anybody*."

Luna and I glanced at each other again. It sounded rather diabolical. Which, in fact, fit right in with what I had learned about Ellie over the past few hours.

"I know it sounds awful that I'm talking about Ellie that way, but whoever did this can't get away with it. Ellie could be really tough to deal with, but she could also be super-caring and loving."

I nodded reflexively, although I hadn't actually seen that side of Ellie at all and was starting to wonder if it really existed at all.

Pris suddenly looked uncomfortable and said, "There's something else, too. I hate to have you think poorly of Ellie, but there was one other thing. I think she was blackmailing this guy who was her friend's husband."

"Frank Morrison?" asked Luna in a solemn voice.

Pris's eyes opened wide. "You know about that?"

"Not really," said Luna hastily. "We just heard a little something, that's all."

Pris nodded. "Small town. All I know is that Ellie was really mad because her friend Judith died in a suspicious manner. She kept telling me there was absolutely no way Judith just took a tumble down the stairs, even if she *had* been drinking at the time. She said Judith had a high tolerance to alcohol because she drank a lot of it, and that Judith was always so coordinated and graceful. Falling down the stairs was not really in her repertoire."

"Ellie thought Judith's husband had something to do with it?" I asked.

"She did. That wasn't just speculation on her part because Judith had told her Frank was abusive. Then, after Judith died and the police ruled it accidental . . . well, now I'm just wondering if maybe Ellie tried to pressure Frank over it," said Pris.

"You think she was blackmailing him?" asked Luna.

Pris shrugged, looking unhappy. "Maybe. I hate saying that, but I wonder if it could explain what happened to her. Maybe she told Frank he had to pay her to stay quiet. She told me he worked at the library, right?"

I said, "As a contractor. He's our tech for the computers."

"Maybe he waited for her to be alone in the library and then killed her," said Pris solemnly.

We paused for a few seconds, thinking this over, then I said, "I'm glad you're going to go to the police with this, Pris."

Pris said, "I feel like I don't really have a choice. I mean, maybe he really didn't have anything to do with Judith's death *or* Ellie's. But what if he did? And the same with Ted Griffith. From what I'm gathering, it sounds like Ellie could have really been exploiting people's secrets. So, yes, I'm definitely going to call Burton back after y'all leave and let him know about this. They might be totally innocent, but I'll feel awful if they're guilty and I didn't say anything to the police about them."

We chatted for a few more minutes, Pris starting to muse over funeral plans. Then we gently took our leave, offering more support from the library if Pris needed it.

Back in her car, Luna said, "That was grim."

I said, "Losing a sibling has got to be hard." I felt the same pang I always did when I mentioned family. I know how I'd felt when my great-aunt had died. She was all the family I'd had left. I couldn't imagine how difficult it must be to lose a sister—someone you'd grown up with, played with, scrapped with.

Luna said, "Oh, I know. But I mean that's on *top* of everything else she's got going on right now. Think about it—Pris is here in Whitby, which is a new town for her. She just moved here because Ellie was here and she needed a place to stay. She's been living with her sister and it was apparently a pretty tough adjustment. She's going through a divorce and a separation from her daughter. She's looking for a job. Now she's lost her sister, who she just argued with. Nothing is going right for her."

I had to agree. Pris must feel like an avalanche had swept over her. "What did you think about what she said about Ted Griffith and Frank Morrison?"

Luna's tone switched from sympathetic to angry. "It sounds like either one of them could have done it. I mean, to a certain degree, Ellie was playing with fire. Don't you think? She never should have been in the situation she was in. I know it sounds like I'm blaming the victim, here, but blackmailing two men?"

I said slowly, "But do you really think she was blackmailing Ted? I agree—it totally sounds like she was blackmailing Frank, especially since we're hearing about it from a couple of different sources. But Ted was over at the library this morning like he was checking in on Ellie. It seemed like he still really cared about her. Maybe she was simply putting pressure on him to leave his wife."

"Like pushing him? And he wasn't really resisting? So maybe he was seriously considering leaving Sunny for Ellie," said Luna. She was quiet for a moment and then said, "So maybe *Sunny* had a motive to get rid of Ellie."

"Because she wanted to keep their family intact?" I asked. "Do they have kids?"

"They don't have children, no. But maybe Sunny wanted to keep her husband for herself—maybe she still really loves him and doesn't want to let him go." But Luna's voice was a little doubtful.

"What's she like?" I asked. "Do you know her? Every time I see her in the library, she seems a little cold."

"Yeah, that's a pretty apt description. I thought that might have been because we were library minions and she's on the board, but it might just be her nature. I probably don't know her any better than you do, but I have seen her out shopping when I've been in town before. I popped over to say hi and her reception was kind of chilly." Luna made a face.

I said, "Do you think Sunny might have a financial motive to stay in a marriage with Ted? Does she have her own independent income?"

"Not as far as I'm aware. She definitely doesn't work, and I don't think she has family money because I remember her family growing up and they were strictly middle-class. So, yeah, it's possible she wants to keep her cushy lifestyle and decided to eliminate the competition."

"What does Ted do?" I asked. "All I know about him is that he was Ellie's Spanish tutor."

Luna snorted. "Sure he was. Nice excuse, anyway. He owns some big I.T. company of some kind . . . computer security or whatnot. I don't know the details, but he's definitely not hurting for money." She glanced over at me. "Then there's Pris, herself. We don't really know her very well, but I like her. You don't think she had anything to do with Ellie's death, do you?"

I shrugged. "They weren't really getting along, from what we've heard and witnessed. But that happens in a lot of families and they don't kill each other over it." I paused. "I thought it was interesting that Pris mentioned Ellie was talking about starting her own business and not being a librarian. I wonder what type of business she was thinking about starting."

Luna snorted. "I'm not so surprised. Ellie didn't seem interested in books in the slightest to me. She'd never have made it as a librarian for very long. Anyway, our conversation with Pris has given us lots to think about." She brightened suddenly, turning to look at me. "Except you don't need to. Because you have a date tonight."

I felt myself color. "Like I said, not really a *date*, Luna. Just an opportunity to catch up with an old friend."

"An old *boy*friend. What are you going to wear?"

"I have no idea," I said with a shrug. I looked down at myself, at my black slacks and white blouse. "I could just—"

"No," said Luna emphatically, shaking her head. "Nope. You're not wearing your work clothes on your date with Connor."

"I could dress them up with some fun jewelry," I protested.

"You don't *have* any fun jewelry. *I* have fun jewelry. Even if we put my fun jewelry into service on your behalf, there's no way to make that outfit look like a date outfit."

I was a little concerned that Luna was going to start suggesting she delve into her own closet to find something for me to wear. Something, no doubt, with way more fuchsia and neon green than I'd ever choose. I hastily said, "I'll go through my closet and find something appropriate."

I somehow ended up promising to send Luna a selfie of me wearing my "date" outfit and got out of the car and into my house.

As I walked in, Fitz was looking mischievous. He rolled onto his back and gave me a teasing look. He *seemed* to be inviting me to rub his furry tummy, but I knew with the expression on his face that he'd bat my hand if I tried to (always without claws, though, since Fitz never wanted to hurt me). Instead, I picked up his favorite toy: the fuzzy chicken-creature on the end of a small fishing pole, and dangled the chicken over him. He immediately exploded into action, hitting the fluffy chicken until I thought it might fall apart.

We played for the next fifteen minutes or so until the cat finally acted like he might be done with the toy and started bathing himself. I gave him a sympathetic look. "Needed to get your extra energy out, didn't you? I know it's been a boring day for you." Usually Fitz had all sorts of social outlets from being in the library. He'd settle in a child's lap and purr approvingly as a beginning reader haltingly read to him. Or he'd cuddle with one of our seniors in the periodical section. I could almost sense everyone's stress dissipate as Fitz ministered to them in his own way. I had no doubt he missed out on all the interaction today and now here I was about to leave on some sort of date. Perhaps.

I pushed the sliding door on my modest closet to inspect my options for supper. There was a veritable sea of browns, blacks, and grays. Actually, considering my budget, I suppose it was more of a creek, not a sea. I frowned. It did look like I was going on a business dinner, and Luna was right—I didn't really have 'fun' jewelry. I swore I had a black skirt, though. I pushed through the hanging clothes, looking to see if there was a straggling skirt that had somehow gotten pushed behind a pair of pants. I finally found it—it had fallen on the floor and was sitting sadly behind a pair of heels that I also never wore. I pulled the skirt out and looked at it doubtfully. It was longer and more shapeless than I remembered and had probably been part of a suit at one time. I figured it was probably the best I could do and took it away for ironing. Then I paired it with a light-blue top that had also gotten buried in the closet and decided it would have to work.

When I saw Connor outside the restaurant, I was glad I'd taken the time to make the extra effort. He was wearing a white golf shirt and khakis that showed off his tan and set off his blond curls. He grinned when he saw me and opened the door to the restaurant saying, "Madame?" as if Quittin' Time was a classy establishment.

We sat down and ordered beers and then appetizers. That bit of business concluded, Connor asked, "So, Ann. When we last left off, we were setting off for different colleges. Catch me up on how things have been since then."

I hesitated. There honestly wasn't a lot of happy, first-date stuff to relate from those years, particularly if this *was* a first date. My college boyfriend had been killed by a drunk driver when he was on his way over to see me. My aunt, who'd raised me, had passed away a few years ago. Plus, I'd just had a colleague murdered in my workplace. This was all going to take some major editing.

"Oh, you know," I said lightly. "Got my degree, then I was able to pick up a master's degree at Whitby College."

"Library science?"

"That's right," I said.

He nodded. "Like I said, I can totally see you over at the library. You always loved books so much. But that's not the only thing that makes you fit well over there. You were incredibly organized when we were in school and I bet that helps you out at work. I remember you lived by that cat planner."

Connor's eyes were twinkling and I grinned at him. "I'd totally forgotten about the cat planner. I had a different one every year." There were always fetching-looking cats and kittens on the front, never aloof cats, and always prettily posed in front of mountains or on the beach or other unlikely places.

"Anytime a teacher even *mentioned* an assignment or a project, you'd immediately pencil it in there. Even before she'd given us all the information or the grading rubric or anything." He took a sip of his drink and leaned back in his chair. "I used to think that made you so incredibly OCD."

"I remember," I said. "So . . . the fact you remember my cat planner makes me think it made a big impression on you."

He gave me a wry look. "I did the same thing all through med school."

"Used a cat planner?" I asked in a teasing voice.

"Well, a planner, anyway. Otherwise, I'd realize at the last minute that everything was due on the same day and I'd have to prioritize what to complete." He shook his head ruefully. "Then I remembered your cat planner and I changed my ways. It made a huge difference. Do you have a cat now?"

I wondered if he thought of me as something of a crazy cat lady. I had the feeling I could tell Connor I had twelve cats and he wouldn't be very surprised. "I have one cat," I said with a smile. "His name is Fitz, short for Fitzgerald. We went in a literary direction with the name, considering, well, he's sort of mine and sort of the library's. But I bring him home from work every night."

He raised his eyebrows. "So he's at the library during the day?"

"Oh, yeah. He loves it. You've never seen a more social cat than Fitz. He's polite about it, too—if a patron isn't a fan of cats, he'll make sure to keep moving until there's someone reaching out for him for a cuddle. He's also really helped with library publicity."

Connor grinned at me. "So he's a social media influencer?"

I chuckled. "I'd love it if I could teach him how to manage his own accounts. He's smart enough that I almost feel he could. The grunt work falls on Luna and me, I'm afraid. But anytime we put out a tweet or an Instagram post or something on Facebook with Fitz's face on it, the post gets more shares and likes than we'd ever seen before. The programs we've hosted have gotten very popular."

Connor said, "Wow, that's great. Somehow I just had a hard time picturing a cat in the library, considering my uncle."

"Your uncle?" I suddenly had the feeling I knew what Connor was going to say next. In fact, there was some long-ago dusty memory that was trying to scratch its way to the surface.

"Wilson. I'm sorry, I thought I mentioned that before. He's the director over there, I think."

Chapter Eight

"He sure is," I said with a laugh. "I'd totally forgotten he was your uncle. I've been working with him for what seems like forever now."

Connor's eyes were curious. "What's it like working with him? I've always liked Wilson, but he's always had such a regimented life. I wondered if he brought that same military-style regiment to the library."

"He likes things orderly, but I do too, so it works out fine for me. He cares a lot about the library and making sure to get the word out about all the things we're doing over there." This always managed to end up giving me a lot of extra work, but I decided not to mention that fact. "But what about you? How did you end up on the medical school track? I remember you were always great at science classes."

Connor said, "You were, too, though. Remember when we were lab partners for A.P. Biology?"

"We had a great teacher for that class and I really enjoyed it. But I never in a million years thought about continuing with science in college."

The waitress brought our spinach and artichoke dip, so we paused for a minute while she set it on the table. Then Connor said, "Mrs. Bowman was a great teacher and she really sparked my interest in science. That's really how it all started. I decided on a biology major and then worked my tail off making sure I had good grades. But like you, I was there on a scholarship and I needed to keep my grades high anyway. Then I just decided to keep on going, took my MCAT, and went off to medical school."

"What was med school like?" I asked.

Connor gave me a wry look. "Hard. And I thought college was hard."

"But you obviously made it through with flying colors," I said lightly.

"I realized I didn't have to have a lot of sleep," he said, grinning at me. "Once I figured that out, I had a lot more time to study."

Connor went on to briefly tell me about his medical residency and the kinds of things he did in emergency medicine. But he came right back to me and the library.

"Now I know who to go to for book recommendations," he said, looking pleased.

I laughed. "Don't tell me you have a ton of time to read, considering all the shifts you're working."

"I don't, but I squeeze it in. I read on my phone, since I have it with me all the time. Right now I'm reading *Being Mortal* by Atul Gawande. Have you read it?"

I nodded. The nonfiction book was by a surgeon and focused on end-of-life care. "Great book. In fact, I was thinking I needed to re-read it. I'd think, as an emergency room doctor, it would be an especially eye-opening read for you."

We talked about books for a while and then, after our entrees arrived, caught each other up on classmates we'd known from high school before moving on to talking about future plans: trips we'd like to take and where we'd like to go with our careers. I was pleasantly surprised because I'd worried we'd just be taking a trip down memory lane. After trading news about old friends, I wasn't sure if we'd have enough in common to really continue the conversation. Instead, we found a lot of common interests and things to talk about. I totally avoided talk of Ellie's murder, thinking that wasn't the kind of thing to be bringing up over dinner with an old friend.

After the meal, we were walking out of the restaurant and Connor laughed. "Speak of the devil," he said in a low voice.

I followed his gaze and saw Wilson there with Mona. Mona was grinning broadly in a way that indicated Luna had filled her in on my date tonight. Wilson, however, looked completely bemused as if trying to figure out why on earth I was standing there with his nephew.

Connor gave Wilson a hug, which Wilson returned rather stiffly. Then Wilson said to Connor and me in a slightly accusatory voice, "I didn't realize the two of you knew each other."

Connor smiled at me and said lightly, "Oh, we're old friends. We went to high school together."

Wilson was apparently too surprised to remember social niceties until Mona cleared her throat. He quickly said, "Connor, this is Mona. Mona, my nephew Connor. He recently moved back to Whitby."

"Good to meet you," said Mona, beaming at him. She gave me a wink, and, to my irritation, I felt a bit of a blush. I felt, somehow, like I was back in high school again and my date was meeting my great-aunt.

"Well, we'll let you get your table. Good to see you, Wilson. Mona, so nice to meet you."

Connor looked behind us to make sure Wilson and Mona were safely out of earshot and then looked at me with big eyes. "Are they *dating*?"

I nodded, grinning. "It's a fairly recent development but they seem to be getting along really well and have more in common than I'd have guessed."

"More in common? Does Wilson even have any interests outside of the library?"

I chuckled. "Well, he likes reading. Mona likes reading, too. And apparently, he has an interest in film that's been recently revived. He presided over our last film club meeting at the library and headed the discussion. Mona likes movies, too."

Connor gave a low whistle. "I'm amazed. It's got to be really good for him to get out of the house and do things. My mom was always a little worried about him—too tied up with his work, you know. He had a couple of relationships in the past, I know, but they just didn't go anywhere. I'm glad he's found someone to go out with."

We got to our cars and I gave him a polite smile and held out my hand to him. Connor gently took my hand and pulled me forward into a hug and kissed me lightly on the cheek. "Good seeing you, Ann. Is it okay if I give you a call and set something up again?"

Apparently, this *was* a date and Luna had been right. "I'd like that, thanks."

We texted our contact info to each other and then Connor waved and drove off in his convertible as I headed for my old reliable Subaru.

As I hopped in my car, I saw Grayson walking out of the newspaper office, looking surprised. He quickly gave me a smile and a wave, which I returned. But I could have sworn I felt his eyes on me as I drove off.

As I was getting ready for work early the next morning, I thought about Grayson. Had he been surprised when he'd seen me with Connor? That anyone else could see me as being something other than friend material? Then I pushed my thoughts about Grayson out of my head—I should be focusing on Connor, who was actually interested in me. Was I interested in Connor, though? I think the thing that piqued my curiosity was just to see where it all led me. It was sort of fun being with someone who seemed totally focused on *me*.

I heard my phone ping with a text message and frowned since it was just six o'clock. I relaxed when I saw it was Wilson telling me the 'tech guy' was coming to help fix the two printers that were on the blink and that he'd be there before the library opened. I texted him back that I was planning on going over there early to fix the bookcase and book situation before hours and I'd be happy to bring the 'tech guy' in.

Of course, the tech guy was Frank. I wasn't actually happy about meeting with him at all, considering I'd just heard a bunch of stuff about how he'd perhaps pushed his wife down the stairs and murdered her. But I *was* interested in finding out where he had been when Ellie was killed, and what his thoughts on Ellie were.

After packing my lunch and eating a quick breakfast, I headed over to the library with Fitz in tow. I got Fitz settled inside the library and then headed outside to remove the signs I'd put up yesterday.

It took me a while to get the library shelves back to normal. The whole time I thought about Ellie, feeling pangs of sympathy for her and muttering a quick prayer as I worked. The shelves weren't too heavy for me to manage without books on them, but they'd have definitely been heavy enough to crush a person fully loaded with volumes. I only hoped she hadn't known what hit her—and that her death had been a quick and fairly painless one. I wondered if Burton could confirm that.

After I got the shelves wrangled, I set to putting the books back on. This took a good deal longer than I had thought since the books were wildly out of order on the floor. I was deep into the process when I heard a knock at the doors, which made me jump. I'd almost forgotten Frank was coming over to fix the printers. Despite wanting to talk to him about Ellie, I felt an underlying sense of revulsion. I was going to have to speak to Burton about what I'd heard and let *him* sort through whether it was something he needed to pursue legally.

Frank waved at me as he saw me approaching the door. He was a big, red-faced, blustery, balding man. Although I'd been upset to hear he might be abusive, I hadn't been really shocked. He had the air of a bully about him, and definitely had a short fuse. I'd heard him getting irritated with the computers, copiers, and printers; muttering under his breath, pounding his big palms against the machines. He'd get even redder in the face than he already was.

"Good morning," he said in a gruff voice, lugging his backpack in one hand. "Thanks for letting me in. Wilson said two of the printers were on the blink."

"As per usual," I said, trying to sound like my regular self with him. "Appreciate you coming by. Having those fixed will make today go a lot smoother."

He walked in, heading toward the computer room, but stopped when he saw the books still mostly on the floor. "Is this where it happened?" he asked in a solemn voice.

"It is," I said, rather brusquely. I didn't like the idea of anyone rubbernecking around the area where Ellie died. "I'm sorting the books out now."

Frank nodded, still looking at the area. "Awful. What a terrible thing to happen here. I hear it wasn't an accident—that she was murdered."

"Did you know Ellie?" I asked.

He shook his head. "Not really. You know, just from doing work here. But she wasn't the kind of person it was easy to get to know, was she? Most of the rest of the staff is friendly and nice to talk to. I mean, Wilson is *fine*, even if he seems distracted most of the time. Luna is always really outgoing, and you'll have a conversation with me."

I gave him a tight smile.

"But Ellie always acted like I was the help. I don't think she was great with the patrons, either. Sometimes she was cheerful and helpful. Other times, she was one step away from snapping at them. But then," he added with a shrug, "it takes all kinds, doesn't it?"

"It does," I said. I cleared my throat. "Did Wilson mention it to you yesterday, then, when he spoke to you about the printers? About Ellie?"

"I knew about it before then," said Frank, dismissively. "I was at home getting ready for work yesterday morning and I had my police scanner on. You hear all kinds of things with a scanner, you know. Usually it's about car accidents, but that's helpful too, since then I can avoid the streets that are backed up. When I heard a call coming in from the library, though, I really stopped and listened. Do they know when it happened?"

I shook my head. "I'm not sure. I know Ellie was locking up night-before-last, so I guess it happened then. She wasn't supposed to be opening up the library in the morning." I tried to keep my expression neutral as I casually said, "I know sometimes your jobs take you around town at all hours. You didn't happen to see anything going on at the library a couple of nights ago, did you?"

He looked regretful. "Nope. I didn't get any calls night-before-last and it wasn't a late night at work, so I was at home just hanging out and watching TV. Maybe the cops will figure out what happened. That has to have set everybody's nerves on edge, having something like that happen in the library. This is supposed to be a safe place."

I said a little coolly, "I think it *is* a safe place. I doubt this was some sort of random act."

Frank raised his eyebrows, either at my chilly tone or at my words. "You think she was targeted somehow? Like somebody was waiting for an opportunity to get rid of her?"

I said, "Maybe, although I don't have any idea why someone would do that."

Frank gave me a doubtful look. "Was Ellie easy to work with?"

I had to force myself not to laugh. Here I was trying to blame Frank for murdering Ellie because I thought she was blackmailing him, and here he was thinking it was me or someone I worked with.

"I wouldn't say she was *difficult* to work with. Ellie was a good librarian and she always got her work done." She wasn't great about taking her breaks on time, but that was hardly grounds for murder.

"What about Wilson? What did he think about her?"

I glanced at the door as if Wilson were sure to come through any moment, wearing his suit and hearing Frank and me discussing his propensity for murder.

"You'd have to ask Wilson that question. In general, Wilson gets along with all his employees, unless they don't show up for work on time."

Frank looked wily for a moment. "Wonder what he'd have thought about one of his librarians scrapping with a library trustee?"

I frowned at him. "What?"

He nodded his head at me. "That's right. I was working on the laptops last week, running updates, and heard Ellie having a nice little argument with Sunny Griffith. You know her, don't you? Kind of an icy-looking blonde. I never thought anybody could get a rise out of that woman, but it sure sounded like Ellie was able to."

I'd witnessed a cold exchange between the two of them the day Ellie died. Did Sunny know Ellie was having an affair with her husband? Was Ellie telling Sunny about it in the hopes Sunny left Ted and she had him to herself?

I said to Frank, "Did you hear what was said?"

He looked regretful. "Not nearly as much as I wanted to. Sunny was sort of hissing and that was hard to hear. But the gist of what I heard was that Ellie was having some sort of a fling with Sunny's husband." He raised his eyebrows at me suggestively.

I suddenly wanted to get as far away from Frank as I could, somehow feeling tainted by association with him. I said, "Be sure to let the police know about that, Frank. That sounds like something Burton should hear about."

"You think Sunny went after Ellie for revenge?" asked Frank, a sort of lurid interest on his face.

"I have absolutely no idea," I said briskly. "Sorry, but I need to get back to putting the shelves back together before the patrons arrive."

Frank nodded, looking morosely toward the printers. "Yeah, I should get started fixing those guys. Okay, well, good talking to you, Ann."

Chapter Nine

I'd finally finished putting the last of the books back on the shelves when Wilson came in. He checked in on Frank's progress first and then headed in my direction. He sighed. "That must have taken a while, Ann. Good work."

I nodded. "All back in place and ready for the day."

Wilson said, "We should likely have some sort of way to memorialize Ellie, considering the circumstances."

I still felt a bit conflicted about Ellie, especially with what I'd heard recently about her blackmailing activities. But Wilson had a point. We couldn't just pretend Ellie's death hadn't happened. I said slowly, "I could come up with a statement for the newsletter and for social media expressing our condolences to Ellie's family. We could ask Pris for a photo. Would something like that work?"

Wilson seemed to have something else on his mind. "Yes, that would work fine, Ann. Just something to show we're not sweeping her death under the carpet, so to speak." He shifted uncomfortably and a red flush rose up from his shirt collar. I had the feeling I knew what was coming next. "So, about last night."

I had to hold back a chuckle at his awkward wording. He was almost making it sound as if he and I had had some sort of romantic encounter, instead of the fact he'd just witnessed me out at a restaurant with his nephew. "Yes?"

Wilson cleared his throat and looked flustered. "Well, you know I'm rather fond of you, Ann. I look at you as sort of a friend instead of a mere employee. A younger friend, but still a friend."

This was sort of sweet in a very floundering way. But still sort of painful to listen to since Wilson looked so uncomfortable. I gave him an encouraging nod.

"It's just . . . how well do you know Connor?" asked Wilson, finally getting around to the point.

I considered this question. "Well, not very well for the last decade or so. He and I did used to date when we were in high school."

"So not very well," said Wilson, latching onto the first part of my answer.

"We had a nice time last night," I said mildly. "We just caught up with each other, remembered old times and old friends. That sort of thing." Wilson was making it sound as if we'd been doing something exceedingly dangerous together—constructing bombs or something.

I waited for him to continue, which he finally did after some hems and haws.

"Connor might be a good sort of person to be friends with," he said. He put some emphasis on the word *friends*.

I nodded, feeling a little sorry for Wilson as he so clearly struggled with making the journey from professional into the personal realm. "He's very interesting. I'd forgotten what a big reader he is, too. We do seem to have some things in common."

Wilson looked rather appalled to hear this. He quickly said, "Oh, I don't really think so, do you? Aside from books, that is. He's in medicine and you're not."

I hid a smile and said, "That's very true."

"And he's very outgoing and you're . . . well, not quite as much."

Wilson was being generous here. He could have gone into 'antisocial' territory. "Again, very true. Wilson, is there a problem with Connor?"

The red flush coming up from his collar spread further up his face. "I wouldn't categorize it as a problem, just a potential shortcoming. Through the years, I've noticed Connor struggling with commitment. That's all, really." He finished up with a look of relief, as if he'd done his duty dissuading me from his nephew. "Well, I should get along to my office now and take a look at my calendar to see what's coming up today."

"What sorts of issues with commitment?" I asked.

Wilson froze and cleared his throat again. "Issues with it? I guess I'd say that he just isn't the serious type. Yes, that's it. He doesn't seem to be a one-woman man, that's all. Which, of course, is not a problem whatsoever if you're not looking for that type of relationship. If you're simply looking for a companion to do things with. Anyway, I did feel compelled to tell you that. From the perspective of a concerned friend." He gave a longing look at his office door and said, "Well, I'd better carry on, then."

As I finished getting the library ready to go, I had plenty of time to think about what Wilson said. In some ways I felt a little defensive about it. I'd never acted as if I was romantically inter-ested in Connor. I thought about my reaction to Connor, and it was none of the heart fluttering or flush of heat I got when Grayson was near. It was more a sense of companionship, and just enjoying being with someone who was interested in being with me. The fun of it all. Who knew where it might go? I wasn't at all sure I wanted it to go any further, anyway. Despite my initial defensiveness, I thought Wilson's protectiveness was very sweet in a fatherly way and was rather touched by it.

When Luna spoke to me, I was so deep into my thoughts that I jumped.

"Sorry!" she said, eyes wide. "Wow, I'm really sorry. I've nev-er seen you so jumpy." She reached out and gave me a quick hug of apology. "Is it because of yesterday morning? Ellie's death must have really gotten to you. But of course it would! Walking into something like that is horrible."

I decided to let her think it was Ellie's death that had put me so deep into thought because telling Luna I was contemplating my potential romantic relationship with Connor would open up a whole other can of worms.

But I shouldn't have thought I was off the hook. Luna said, "Let's talk about other things. How did it go with Connor last night? Mom said she saw you out with him last night."

I nodded and gave her a wry look. "We did see them out. I'd totally forgotten that Wilson is Connor's uncle."

Luna snorted. "Isn't that the craziest? I didn't know it either until Mom came home and told me. Anyway, how *was* it? I know you always say your dates are super-awkward. Was that what this one was like?"

"Actually, it was totally the opposite. Very low-key. Connor has the gift of gab, I think, too—he did a great job making me feel at ease." It was more than making me feel at ease—he had the way of making me feel there wasn't anyone else he'd rather be with at that moment than you.

Luna made a face. "I mean, I'm glad it wasn't awkward, but I was hoping there might be more of a spark happening. Feeling at ease is all well and good, but feeling a *spark* is a lot better when you're on a date." She frowned. "You *were* on a date, weren't you?"

"I wasn't sure at first," I admitted. "But later in the evening, I got the impression I was."

Luna put a hand to her heart. "But you did dress up, right? You never sent me a selfie showing me your outfit."

"That's because I really need to go shopping for clothes that aren't work clothes. But yes, I did manage to find something to put on. When we were leaving, he said he wanted to do it again sometime soon."

"Then we need to go shopping sometime soon," said Luna decisively. "Like after work tonight."

I demurred. "Maybe we can do it this weekend, Luna. Besides, I don't want to drag you out shopping after a long day at work."

"Drag me? There's no dragging needed, Ann. You may not realize this, but I live to shop."

I made a face. "Yeah, that's not so much my thing. Even if it was my thing, I don't have the budget to indulge it."

Luna wagged her finger at me. "That's what I thought you'd say. That's why I need to introduce you to my most favorite place in the world."

I shifted uncomfortably, looking at Luna. She and I had totally different ways of approaching our wardrobe. Her approach was all about fun and color and texture. Mine was all about practicality and neutrals and having clothes that coordinated with other clothes. I couldn't imagine a place where she and I could shop together and find things we both were interested in.

She laughed at my expression, which was apparently a dead giveaway. "No, you're going to like it, Ann. It's a consignment shop and it has a ton of different options and really good quality stuff. It's run by the Junior League and people donate things to it all the time. It's the Nearly New Shoppe."

I frowned. "Why haven't I noticed it in town?"

"It's not in town. It's a town over but it's only fifteen minutes away. They'll be open until seven and I know we're both off at five today. Let's do it!"

I knew that determined gleam in her eye and realized I didn't have a chance and might as well just give in. "All right. We'll go at five."

Luna grinned at me. "Well, try not to be too excited, Ann. Wow. Anyone would think you were going to your own hanging."

The day sped by far too quickly for my liking. There were, of course, a lot of curious patrons asking why the library had been closed the day before. I tried to give as straightforward an answer to that as I could, but it still created shockwaves through the community. Talking about poor Ellie over and over again was also playing havoc with my stress levels. It probably didn't help when Burton entered in his uniform and came over to talk to me at the circulation desk.

"You realize you're probably making me look like Suspect #1," I said lightly.

"Are you?" he asked, just as lightly. "You did work with Ellie. And you and Luna didn't seem too pleased with her. I probably should be taking a look at your alibi."

I made a face. "Unfortunately, my alibi is nonexistent unless you can figure out how to make Fitz talk."

Which was exactly when Fitz bounded over and up on the circulation desk, giving Burton a very earnest mew.

He chuckled and scratched Fitz under the chin. "I think he just gave one."

"Seriously, though, it's true that Ellie wasn't our most favorite coworker. That's something I'm not feeling especially good about right now, considering what happened. But it was all due to her workplace shenanigans."

Burton raised his bushy eyebrows. "Shenanigans, were they?"

"Just the usual—taking breaks at the wrong time, not coming back promptly from lunch or not leaving for lunch at the right time. That sort of thing." I glanced around quickly to make sure no one was in earshot and said, "I'm glad you're here because I was going to call you later."

"Sounds like you've heard something," said Burton, brightening. "My favorite library sleuth is on the job again."

"Well, I'm not sure about that, but I did have the chance to get out and about a little yesterday with the library being closed.

There were a couple of things I thought I should pass along in case you haven't heard them yourself."

"That's good. Because the lab was able to confirm it was murder," said Burton in a grim tone. "Fortunately, it sounds like Ellie expired immediately, so she shouldn't have suffered at all. Just the same, I'm eager to find out who's behind it all. What have you got?"

I shifted uncomfortably and glanced in the direction of the computer room, although Frank had already fixed the printer problems and taken his leave. "Well, the first thing I heard is about Frank Morrison. Apparently, Ellie might have had a proclivity to blackmailing people. At least, I've heard of two people who were victims."

Burton's eyes opened wide. "A blackmailing librarian?"

"It sure looks that way. So Frank Morrison's wife was a friend of Ellie's and told her Frank was abusive. Then she fell down the stairs at her home and died as a result of her injuries."

Burton said slowly, "Ellie figured Frank had probably shoved her down the stairs. That it wasn't an accident. I remember that case. We ruled foul play hadn't been involved."

"Why would anyone think so unless they knew his wife was being abused? Anyway, from what I hear, Ellie was blackmailing Frank over it."

Burton took out his little notebook and jotted down a few notes. "Hm. And you said there might be another blackmail victim, too?"

"Tara Fuller. She works down at the coffee shop. A patron here told me he'd overheard Ellie trying to put pressure on Tara out in the parking lot recently. Luna and I went over to Keep

Grounded and Tara admitted Ellie was trying to force her to pay her money to keep quiet about a prescription drug addiction Tara had. At the time, Tara worked at the hospital. Now she's a barista and is no longer using prescription drugs." I really felt like a snitch, but I figured it would be best to tell Burton everything and let him sort it out. "She won't get into any trouble, will she?"

"Tara?" Burton shook his head. "Not unless she's involved in Ellie's death, that is. It sounds like Ellie made some enemies in the short time she's been here in Whitby."

I said, "There's something else, too. You know the guy who drove up to talk to us yesterday morning at the library?"

"Ted Griffith?" asked Burton with another lift of his eyebrows. "Let me guess—he was romantically entangled with Ellie."

"Police intuition?" I asked, grinning at him.

"Something like that. Maybe a sixth sense from being a cop for so many years. Plus, his explanation didn't exactly ring true. Spanish lessons?" Burton snorted.

I shrugged. "Well, maybe they started out that way, but they sure didn't seem to end up that way. Ellie's sister believed them to be having an affair. I've heard that Ted's wife, Sunny, might have had a run-in with Ellie over it."

Burton frowned. "So Sunny found out that Ellie was having an affair with her husband?"

I said, "It sounded more like Ellie was *telling* Sunny about the affair because she wanted her to leave Ted so he was available for a real relationship with her. Ellie might have pressured Ted beforehand, telling him if he didn't leave his wife that she'd inform Sunny about the affair."

"That sort of falls in line with her interest in blackmailing. She wanted Ted for herself and decided to ensure she got him." Burton jotted down more notes. "Let me know if you hear anything else. And thanks for this, Ann."

Chapter Ten

The rest of the day was a blur and I was surprised when Luna came up to me, car keys in her hand and looking impatient. "Come on, Ann! It's time to head out."

I looked at her vaguely and then at my watch. "Five o'clock already?" I know I didn't sound exactly happy about it.

"It will be six o'clock by the next time you remember to glance at your watch unless you get out of here."

Luna was right. I sometimes ended up either getting caught up with research requests from patrons or other distractions and managed to lose track of time. I closed the tabs and the document I was working on and collected my things. Then I called for Fitz and he came bounding up from the direction of the children's area.

"I'll just run Fitz by the house and meet you there," I said, putting Fitz in his carrier.

"Oh, no. I'm not going to take the chance that you go inside your house and find a great excuse not to go shopping. I'll follow you home and take you in my car."

And that's how it happened. I got Fitz settled at home with a bowl of cat food, gave him a quick rub, and hopped in the car with Luna for the trip to Nearly New. Fifteen or twenty minutes later, she pulled up in front of a small, brick building shaded by large trees. There were quite a few cars there already. I was somewhat relieved by the displays in the window which showed tailored professional clothes in neutral colors.

"This actually looks like a great place to shop," I said to Luna.

She knit her eyebrows together in a ferocious expression. "I saw you eyeing the clothes in the window. Those are work clothes and the whole reason we're here is to get you something cute and fresh. If you want to get work clothes *too*, then fine. But we're going to stay on task." She had a devilish glint in her eyes which I attributed to her plan to make me leave my fashion comfort zone.

Luna was proving to be quite the taskmaster when it came to shopping. As soon as we got inside, she went right over to a rack filled with "fun colors." In fact, the entire store was sorted by color instead of by size or style, so we'd go to a rack filled with pink hues and then find my size.

I was studying a selection of clothes in a quiet shade of gray-blue when Luna hissed to me, "Don't look now, but Sunny Griffith is volunteering here today."

I was careful not to immediately look, but when I did, I spotted her at the checkout counter, sorting clothes that had been brought in into different piles. I remembered Luna's devilish look and said, "You must have had a good idea she was going to be here since you've shopped here before."

Luna looked pleased with herself. "I've seen her here before and thought we might want to do a little investigating while you shop. She's a bit long in the tooth to be a regular member. She must be a sustainer and just enjoys volunteering here."

I smiled to myself. Luna read a lot of Nancy Drew books as a child and clearly still relished the idea of being part of an investigation. It was another reason why she and Burton would make such a good match if she would just open her eyes.

It was truly a pleasant shop. There was old pop music from the 70s playing softly in the background and the assorted clothes were in pleasing shades. The shop was well-organized and bright and cheery and there were a good number of women who were looking through the selection. Plus, you couldn't beat the fact it was all consignment and the prices fit my budget. It definitely didn't seem a bad place to volunteer.

Luna steered me toward some clothes that fit in with her sense of fun but weren't too crazy for me. The colors were bright but not over the top, and the style was straightforward. I walked over to Sunny to see if I could try them on in one of the three fitting rooms at the back of the room.

Sunny looked up at me distracted, her blonde hair falling over her face. As she absently pushed it away, she gave me a surprised look. "Hi there! It's Ann, isn't it? Sorry, I should definitely know everyone at the library, being on the board, but somehow I'm not as good with names as I should be." She looked solemn suddenly. "I think Wilson mentioned to me that you were the one who found Ellie yesterday morning. I'm so sorry."

I nodded, looking serious. "We feel awful about what happened to Ellie. It's been quite a week."

Sunny nodded back, her face carefully emotionless. "It really must have been. And now you're maybe doing some shopping to try to cheer up a little?"

I gave her a wry look. "It's more that my coworker Luna has decided I need to wear more color, at least in terms of my casual-wear wardrobe. I might possibly have a date in my future and everything I have at home is pretty . . ."

"Dry and boring?" chirped Luna from behind me.

"I was going to say *neutral*."

Sunny was wearing neutrals herself, a tan skirt and black top that I had a feeling did not come from Nearly New. She nodded and gave me a considering look. "You could get away with neutrals for your date if you had some fun jewelry to make them seem a little less professional."

"Apparently, I don't own any fun jewelry," I said dryly, remembering the state of my jewelry box.

Sunny continued looking thoughtfully at me as if I were a puzzle to figure out. "Got it. All right, so let's do two things. Let's find fun jewelry for future dates and outings so you can go from work to evening quickly and let's try and find a few pieces that are a bit brighter on the color palette. How do you feel about patterns?"

My expression must have shown exactly how I felt about patterns because Sunny chuckled. "I see."

Luna rolled her eyes. "For heaven's sake, Ann. Just try something on. You might find you really like it. That's the great thing about trying stuff on—you can see different versions of yourself and decide whether you like them or not. Patterns can be very subtle. It doesn't mean you have to wear big stripes or something."

Sunny said, "I do have a few prints that I've been eyeing. One has tiny dots on a navy background and one is a small floral pattern on a black background. One's a blouse you can wear with your neutral slacks and the other is a dress."

Luna clasped her hands together. "A dress!"

I ended up taking both back into the changing room to try them on. While I was in there, Luna and Sunny managed to locate a lemon-colored top, a green blouse, and some other prints and colors. A few times I came out of the dressing room to show them (Luna seemed to like everything) and a few times the vision in the mirror in front of me was so bad that I didn't leave the dressing room at all.

I finally decided on both the dot and floral prints and the lemon-colored blouse. Then I was handed an assortment of jewelry to liven up my usual outfits. I ended up with a pair of drop earrings, stacked bangle bracelets, and a multicolored necklace. Luna picked up a few things, too.

It looked like a lot of stuff and I sort of held my breath as Sunny rang it all up. When she told me they were all just $25, I let the breath out in relief. I was definitely going to have to come back to Nearly New.

As I pulled my debit card out, Sunny said, "Have you heard anything else about Ellie? I'm planning on going to the funeral service, of course."

Luna and I glanced at each other. I said, "I haven't heard anything about the service, no. I did speak with her sister yesterday and it sounded like she was starting to plan something, but I don't know when it's going to be."

Sunny nodded absently and then said, "Have you heard if the police have any leads? It did sound as if it was a deliberate act and not an accident."

I shook my head. "I don't know. I'm sure Burton will conduct a very thorough investigation."

Luna, never one to beat around the bush, said, "They're thinking it happened that night around the time the library was closing. Were you out and about then?"

Sunny gave her a startled look and Luna continued with a laugh, "I mean, were you out where you might have witnessed anything going on at the library? I'm starting to think no one goes out in this town after eight o'clock."

Sunny said slowly, "No, I'm afraid I was at home and didn't see anything at all." She gave me a tight smile. "I hope you enjoy your new clothes, Ann, and that you have a good time on your date."

That definitely seemed like a dismissal.

Back in the car, I mused, "You know, she definitely doesn't seem like a *Sunny*, which implies something far lighter and happier."

"*Reserved* is the word that comes to mind," said Luna with a snort. "I guess that's not a name, though." She glanced over at me. "I thought it was interesting that she acted like she really didn't know Ellie. Like she was just some random new librarian and not a woman trying to ruin her life by breaking up her marriage."

"Well, that's hardly something she was going to bring up with us, was it? She knows us on a professional level, after all. She wasn't going to start spewing out her personal life to us. That would be weird."

Luna said, "True. But I think the way she was acting was even weirder. She's going to go to Ellie's funeral as if she's someone who cared about her?"

"She has to act like any other trustee. Sunny wouldn't want to draw attention to herself. She's probably hoping no one knows about her interactions with Ellie. But that's where she's wrong."

Luna said, "I thought I spotted you with Burton earlier. Did you fill him in?"

"I did. I figured he could sort through all the information I had and make sense out of it. I mean, maybe some of the stuff we heard is off-track but it's not *our* responsibility to separate the truth from the lies, is it?" I frowned over at Luna. It was a point that was bothering me a little. I didn't like implicating people I knew, but I liked keeping damaging information to myself even less.

Luna said stoutly, "You did the right thing, Ann. You mentioned Frank Morrison, I hope? That was so messed up. I hope Burton throws the book at him." She pulled into my driveway.

"Can he, though? For one thing, it's hearsay. For another, the source of the hearsay is dead. There weren't any witnesses."

Luna said, "There's got to be something he can do. Maybe he can catch Frank off-guard during an interview and get him to admit to it. Anyway, I'm not happy with him working at the library, under the circumstances."

"I was going to mention it to Wilson, but I haven't had a chance yet." I still felt a little uneasy about it, considering it was basically just a rumor, but I felt like Wilson needed to at least know and then he could decide for himself. Frank wasn't a full employee, after all, just a contract worker.

I suddenly felt very tired. Whether it was because I felt I was suddenly surrounded by people with questionable ethics or whether it was because going shopping had been exhausting, I had no idea.

Luna apparently picked up on it. "Hey, you look wiped. Why don't you go in and lie down for a while and snuggle with Fitz? You've got something to eat for supper, right?"

I did still need to make a run to the grocery store, but I just didn't feel up to it right then. "I think I can make myself a can of tomato soup or a grilled cheese sandwich. I'll be fine. I'm mostly just tired, not hungry."

Luna appeared to be getting into maternal mode. "Stay hydrated and get some rest. You know, you don't *have* to come in tomorrow. You could call Wilson and he'd totally understand."

I shook my head. "I'd be worse just moping around home the whole day. Better to stay distracted and keep busy, right?" I opened the car door and stepped out, gathering my bags and giving her a wave. "Thanks for all your help."

I went in and started a load of laundry of my new, used, clothes and then sat down on the sofa to cuddle Fitz, who'd been watching me solemnly as I started the washer. I read for a little while, then turned on the TV to watch the news. The news, however, stressed me out, so I switched it off and opted to head off to bed after putting my things in the dryer. It felt good to be stretched out with Fitz curled up next to my side. Soon, I fell into a deep sleep.

The next morning, I woke up feeling refreshed. I showered and then looked in my closet to pull out one of the outfits that I thought of as my "uniform" for work. But then I hesitated. Maybe a change would cheer me up a little. I ran the dryer again for a few minutes to get the wrinkles out that had set in overnight and then pulled out the lemon-colored blouse and paired it with a couple of bangles, hoping they wouldn't drive me too crazy as I typed at work during the day.

When I arrived with Fitz at the library, Luna was already there, preparing for her early storytime with the toddler crowd. When she spotted me, her eyes opened wide.

"A date? Tonight?" she asked.

"No and no," I said lightly. "I just thought I'd give some of my new things a spin, that's all. I haven't heard from Connor at all, nor did I expect to." This wasn't completely true, only because he seemed so determined to follow up with me to set our next outing up. But it wasn't as if I was dwelling on it.

Luna frowned. "Well, he might be trying to just give you a little space. He wouldn't want to act as if he was coming on too strong. I'm glad you're brightening up your work clothes! You're going to make us all smile today . . . that lemon is pretty cheerful."

She hurried off to finish setting up the storytime as the first toddlers and moms filed in and I dove into my emails.

I rubbed my head as I saw there were two already asking about the tech drop-in. It had to be really frustrating for the patrons who were having trouble with their computers—in this day and age, it could really mess you up on a number of levels not to be able to communicate or get information like you wanted to. I sent an email to Timothy to ask him what his availability looked like so I could send an answer along to the patrons as to the date for the event. Then I started working on the column I wrote for the newspaper on behalf of the library.

That's what I was deeply engrossed in when I heard someone say my name. I jumped and then smiled sheepishly at Grayson, who had apparently been standing right in front of me for some time.

"Sorry," I said. "I'm actually working on the column for you and obviously got a little too absorbed in it."

He grinned at me. "Hey, I'm glad to see you take it so seriously. Not that I ever had any doubt, though."

"Did you need anything?"

"No, just saying hi. I'm here to do some research on a story about Whitby's history and just thought I'd run by the desk. Oh, and did you want to plan a day for our picnic and hike?"

"Sure, just let me pull my calendar up so I can see what my work schedule looks like." I got my phone out and opened the calendar app. While I was doing that, I heard my name again, a different voice this time.

It was Connor, looking pleased to see me and giving me that confident smile of his as he stood there in his scrubs. "Hey, Ann," he said. "Just getting off a shift and thought I'd stick my head in and see if you wanted to catch supper with me again."

I watched curiously as Grayson's mouth tightened into a displeased frown. He didn't seem to like Connor very much. I'd like to think it had something to do with me, but after so much time spent in just-friends territory, I suspected it might be something else.

Connor, at any rate, seemed either oblivious or immune to his dislike. He stuck his hand out and said, "Hi, I'm Connor." He smiled his impish smile, blue eyes dancing.

Grayson grunted and rather reluctantly extended his own hand. "Grayson."

"Good to meet you!" said Connor warmly before turning back to me. "What do you say, Ann? Free tonight? How late are you working?"

"Just until six tonight and then I'll have to run Fitz back home. But supper would be great," I said.

"Wonderful," he said, flashing his sparkly grin at me again. "Sorry to interrupt you guys. See you later, Ann."

Grayson watched Connor as he practically skipped out the building and headed for his sports car. "I don't think I've seen him around town. Is he new here?"

"New and not-new at the same time. He grew up here in Whitby, but then left to go to school and have his residency."

"A doctor, then." Grayson crinkled up his forehead. "Well, that explains the car and the scrubs. Did you know him when you were growing up?"

Grayson had only been in Whitby for the last year or two. I said lightly, "Yes, we were friends. Actually, we dated for a while when we were in high school. We've been catching up."

"That's nice," said Grayson a little stiffly.

"Anyway, back to the hike and picnic," I said. "It looks like I have some free time on Sunday, if that works for you?"

Grayson still looked rather bemused as if he'd totally lost his focus. "Right. Sunday works for me, too. I'll call you and set up a time later."

"Okay, sounds good." I watched him head out of the library and then tried to get back into my column for the newspaper.

When Luna checked back in with me late in the afternoon after we'd both had a busy day, she said, "Want to go grab some food out? I saw the deli was having a buy-one-get-one-half-off."

"I would, but Connor ran by here a while ago and asked me to dinner. I guess I'll just focus on my leftovers in the breakroom," I said. Then I smiled as Luna's face lit up.

"He did? Why didn't you say so earlier? It's that lemon-colored top, I'm telling you. He couldn't resist you."

I shrugged and gave a laugh. "Whatever. Like I said, I still think we're mostly just friends. At any rate, it's fun to go out and do things."

Luna said with a frown, "Didn't I see Grayson come in earlier, too?"

I scooped up Fitz, who had seen me collecting my things and knew it must be time for us to go home. "Yes, he came by to set up our hike and picnic."

Luna's eyebrows flew up. "Really? I'm sensing a love triangle."

"Your senses are sadly off. Malfunctioning, actually. Grayson and I, as usual, are doing something strictly as friends and so that he can write a story on local hikes for the paper."

Luna looked disappointed. "We really could use a love triangle, you know. It would liven up things at the library."

I put Fitz in the cat carrier and said, "As far as this dinner goes tonight, I'm mostly just trying to be open to see where things lead. Connor is easy to be with and it's kind of flattering to get the attention, to be perfectly honest. If nothing else, he's fun to be with."

Luna said, "Go have fun. If anybody deserves it, you do."

Chapter Eleven

After taking Fitz back home and feeding him, the phone rang. It was Connor, sounding regretful. "I hate this, but a coworker asked me to trade shifts with him because he's having some sort of family emergency. I'm so sorry."

"No worries, Connor. That's nice of you to step in like that. Didn't you just get *off* a long shift, though?"

"Afraid so. But I did have a few hours in-between and took a nap and a shower, so it's not as bad as it could be. I mostly feel bad about supper. Can we take a raincheck?"

I said, "Of course we can. Anytime."

As I hung up, I reflected that part of me did feel a very mild disappointment. But part of me was relieved to just spend a quiet evening at home with some mac and cheese, my book, and Fitz. I wondered if I'd have had the same reaction if it had been Grayson.

A couple of days went by, thankfully uneventfully. I sent Grayson over the column I'd written for the newspaper full of book recommendations and upcoming library events—and was even able to mention the tech drop-in date, since I'd coordinated a date with Timothy for that. Connor and I didn't have the supper, but we did have lunch and it was just as fun as our first outing together had been, with lots of laughing and reminiscences.

Then things got quite a bit more solemn as the date for Ellie's funeral came. Wilson had coordinated the schedule so he and I could both be there as representatives for the library. He felt positive there would also be a couple of library trustees, if not more. The day was blustery and gray and seemed fit for a funeral, especially one for a young person. When Wilson and I arrived at the cemetery for the graveside service, Pris was already there, speaking with the funeral director and looking pale and drawn.

Wilson murmured to me, "I suppose we'll stand in the back, to make room for family under the tent."

I nodded. "Although I got the impression Ellie and Pris didn't have much remaining family. But let's stand farther back, to be on the safe side."

Because Ellie was relatively new to town and Pris was *very* new to town, there was just a small trickle of mourners who came in. When Pris spotted Wilson and me standing back behind the tent, she spoke to the funeral director, who came over.

"If everyone could come sit under the tent, please? There will be plenty of room for all," he said with a studied solemn and efficient manner.

Wilson and I moved and sat in the back row under the tent and others followed until there were at least a smattering of mourners there. I noted with surprise that Sunny Griffith was there with Ted. He wore a dark suit and a grim expression and seemed to be perspiring more than the day warranted. Sunny was wearing a brown dress and was holding onto Ted's arm.

Wilson murmured, "That's nice of her to come. I was hoping there'd be a bit more attendance from the library board. At least we have one trustee here."

The service was short, but nice. The minister read Psalm 23, there was a hymn we joined in, and then the minister said a few words. After it ended, Wilson and I walked up to speak with Pris, who seemed completely drained. She gave us a tight smile and thanked us for coming. There didn't appear to be any sort of funeral reception afterward, which was understandable under the circumstances and with Pris being so new to town.

Sunny and Ted walked over to join us.

"It's good of you to have come, Sunny," said Wilson after shaking their hands.

Sunny said smoothly, "Of course—I wanted to be here. Such an awful thing to have happened and to such a young person."

Ted pulled at the collar of his button-down, still perspiring and looking extremely uncomfortable, despite the wind and the grayness of the day. But, if what I'd heard was true, he was at the funeral of a woman he'd been close with. He could be grieving and no one would be comforting him over her death because their relationship had been illicit. It was enough to make anyone look rough.

Sunny apparently picked up on how bad he looked, too. She gave him a sharp look and said, "Unfortunately, Ted ate something that didn't agree with him last night."

"Sorry to hear that," said Wilson gruffly.

Ted gave a rather sick-looking smile in acknowledgement and swallowed hard.

"But he was determined to come to the funeral with me and support me today," said Sunny smoothly. "As soon as we get you back home, though, you should get some rest, Ted. Health is so important, isn't it? And it's something you don't really appreciate until you don't have it. I've made a goal recently to move more. I feel as if I find myself sitting all day long. I've got a smartwatch now that reminds me when I need to start moving."

It felt like an abrupt segue to another subject, which made me wonder if Sunny was trying to maneuver the conversation away from Ted.

I said ruefully, "I've made the same goal in the past and have had a hard time sticking to it. Maybe I should get one of those watches, too. It's not as if I couldn't get up from the desk and start shelving books. There are *always* books to be shelved."

"Oh, we've all made promises to ourselves about moving more," said Sunny, making a face.

Ted said, apparently trying to make an effort to finally speak, "That's why Sunny and I have decided to start small. We figured if we set the bar really low that we might be able to form a habit."

Sunny gave him a fond smile. "We're walking in the park every day. We're not trying to jog or anything. Not saying we're going to spend an hour out there. Just making the time to go there and do *something* every day regularly. Although, we may have to take a pass today, under the circumstances." She looked at me again. "I've been reading the columns Grayson has been writing for the newspaper on good local hikes. I understand from reading them that you're the local guide for him on the hikes."

"Oh, I think 'guide' isn't really the right word for it. I'm just familiar with a bunch of them because that's what I liked to do as a teenager. It's been fun to introduce the trails to a newcomer."

Sunny glanced at Ted. "Maybe we can work our way up to those."

"Yes, but let's tackle the park first," he said with a laugh. "It's at least flat."

Wilson brought up some business to do with the library board as Ted wandered off to sit down on a shady bench nearby. Sunny gave him a concerned look as she spoke with Wilson. A few minutes later, she and Ted left the cemetery and Wilson and I followed at some distance behind.

Wilson gave a sigh as we got into his car. "Well, that's done," he said in the manner of someone checking something off a mental list. "We can feel good about attending the funeral, Ann. Poor Ellie is laid to rest. Hopefully at peace, although I'm sure she'd rest better if her killer were brought to justice." He glanced over at me as he drove toward the library. "Have you heard any updates from the police at all? I know you sometimes speak with Burton."

"I haven't heard anything but I'm sure he's working hard to find out who's behind her death."

Wilson shifted in his seat, looked at me and then looked back at the road. I had the feeling we were about to suffer through another uncomfortable conversation. "Listen, about Connor," he started. Then he sighed and continued, "I'm sorry,

I shouldn't have gotten involved in your business. He's a fine young man, really. I'm sure he's nice to spend time with. I've always been fond of him when I've seen him at holiday gatherings and that sort of thing."

I waited for him to continue, which he did after some hemming and hawing. "It's just that he's never seemed to want to really settle down or even commit. He's left a string of broken hearts in his wake. I just didn't want to see that happen to you and I spoke out of turn."

I said sincerely, "Wilson, I appreciate your looking after me, I really do."

"It's just that you don't have . . . well, you don't have any family to advise you on such things. I know it wasn't my place to step into that role, but I couldn't seem to help myself." Wilson looked so exasperated with himself that I nearly laughed.

Instead, I said warmly, "I'm glad you stepped out of line. You're welcome to do that at any time. You shouldn't worry—like I said, Connor and I aren't anything serious. We're just enjoying going out with each other and having meals."

He looked both relieved and pleased at this and said, still flustered, "Excellent! That's good. Like I said, he's very good company, of course, and if anyone deserves a break it's you, Ann. You work very hard." At the mention of work, his mind reverted back into professional mode and he said, "So, this technology drop-in. I'm curious to hear how that's going to go. It's such a different set-up than our usual class format."

So we talked about that for a few minutes on the drive back to the library and I was glad for the change of subject. Neither of us were comfortable talking about personal things to each other, as was evident in the fact that he really never brought Mona up in my presence. I told him that the drop-in date was set, Timothy was available to help out, and it had been duly advertised on social media.

"Good," said Wilson briskly. "I suppose Timothy is a volunteer, then? I was going to suggest our tech guy, Frank Morrison, but we'd have to pay him to participate."

"Actually, I've been meaning to talk with you about Frank," I said slowly.

Wilson frowned. "Has something happened? I thought he did good work for us."

"Oh, he does. At least, when he's left, everything he's worked on seems to be in good shape. It's just that I've heard something about Frank, and it's left me a little conflicted. I wasn't sure what I should make of it, so I thought I'd tell you about it and let you decide."

I told Wilson what I'd heard about him, stressing again that it was second or third-hand knowledge.

Wilson looked grim as he pulled into a parking spot at the library. "Well. That's not good." He paused. "Honestly, it doesn't speak well of Ellie, either. Am I to understand she was probably blackmailing Frank with the information she had? I suppose this means Frank had an excellent motive for murdering Ellie, considering she was extorting him."

"I did tell Burton about it, just to fill him in. That's exactly why I wanted to let you know, keeping in mind this is basically hearsay."

Wilson frowned and opened his car door absently, but stopped again before getting out of the car. "I'm glad you told me, Ann. I'll have to consider this very seriously. Frank is, after all, a contract worker for the library and we could simply use another tech service until Burton works this all out. Or, perhaps, we won't have any other issues on our end that need to be resolved until then."

I nodded somewhat doubtfully. Our copier was notorious for going out and seemed to take great pleasure in its regular malfunctioning. I had the feeling Wilson was going to have to come up with his decision sooner than later.

As it happened, though, the next morning, I had a visit from Burton at home. With a grim face he said, "Ann, just wanted to let you know we discovered Frank Morrison's body last night."

I invited Burton inside and poured him a cup of coffee, topping off my own cup too. We sat down at my tiny kitchen table. I quietly said, "What happened?"

Burton rubbed his tired eyes with his hand. "Frank was murdered. Shot. A fisherman found his body early this morning in the lake."

He and I sat quietly for a few moments while I tried to absorb this. I sighed. "It just doesn't make any sense, does it? I was wondering if maybe Frank had been the one to murder Ellie since he seemed to have the most pressing motive. I thought he'd tried to hush her up for good to make sure she didn't spill the beans about his abusive marriage."

Burton nodded. "That was sort of the direction my mind was going in, too. Now, I know he did contract work at the library sometimes. They told me you were off today, so that's why I'm here. Did Frank say anything to you lately that might have provided any clues as to who might have wanted to kill him?

Has he been feuding with anybody? Mentioned any relationships? Problems he's had?"

I considered this and then shook my head regretfully. "No. Honestly, I wasn't too jazzed about talking with him to begin with, knowing what I knew about him. It was the morning after I'd found Ellie in the library and he and I were alone so I was still re-shelving books and getting everything ready for us to open to the public. Maybe I should have tried to get him to open up more but I was feeling kind of leery around him."

"No, you were fine, Ann. Considering he was a suspect and you were alone in the library with him, you were smart not to press him for information. I'm wondering now if he did know something, though—something somebody didn't want to have exposed."

"Was Frank murdered at the lake, then?" I asked slowly. "It just sort of seems like an unusual place for him to be."

Burton said, "You don't think he'd have headed out there for recreation's sake? There are trails around the area, too."

I shrugged. "It's not like I knew Frank really well, but he'd always seemed like more of an indoor person to me. He was very into computers, of course, and not just for his work—he's talked before about the video games he played and stuff like that. He was interested in our film club, although he never made a meeting."

"Seems like an odd conversation to have with a librarian," said Burton with a chuckle.

I gave him a wry look. "I guess it does. It was when he was fixing one of our laptops at the library and I was helping a patron with another one. The patron was actually interested in getting a game for his grandson for his birthday and that's what made Frank offer his opinions on them." I took another sip of my coffee, feeling as if I needed to be a little more alert this morning than I currently was. "So Frank's body was discovered this morning—do you know the last time he was seen?"

"Apparently, his neighbor saw him leaving his house around eight-thirty last night," said Burton.

"Do you have any idea when he must have been killed?"

Burton said, "It's still a little sketchy because of the water, but we're thinking sometime late last night or very early this morning. Unfortunately, we haven't had any luck so far nailing down the time. It's a fairly remote area of the lake and there apparently wasn't anyone on the walking trails—not that late at night anyway. It almost seems as if Frank deliberately picked that area."

"Which goes back to your wondering if maybe he knew something about Ellie's death and had to be silenced," I said.

"It's just total speculation at this point," said Burton, rubbing his face again tiredly. "But yeah, I can't help but think maybe he was unwisely meeting up with the killer. Maybe to get money in exchange for his silence. At any rate, I appreciate your thoughts on him. He sure doesn't sound like the kind of guy who's going to go take a midnight run for his health."

I shook my head.

"Okay, well I should be getting along and leaving you to your day off."

"Do I need to keep quiet about Frank's death?" I asked.

"No, no. The newspaper was already at the scene asking questions and I'm sure it's already being talked about around town. Do let me know if you hear anything please. I'm ready to put this case to bed. And then put *myself* to bed," he said with a dry laugh. "I feel like I haven't gotten good sleep for ages."

After Burton left, I kept thinking about Frank. I decided to change my plans for my day off. But considering my plans had previously consisted of snuggling with Fitz and reading *This Tender Land*, I figured I could change them easily enough.

For one thing, I felt like I could stand to get out of the house. For another, I'd been telling myself I needed to get some more exercise and work that into my days off instead of just lying around the house. But the truth was that after Burton told me about Frank, I felt a real restlessness and felt like I needed to talk to someone and sort of work through it all. Luna came to mind, but I knew she was working today. I was sure Grayson was at the newspaper office but thought I might check in with him later after I'd exercised. I decided on more coffee first . . . and then thought about Tara. She'd been so open to talk through things when Luna and I had last seen her.

So I left Fitz happily curled up in a sunbeam on the kitchen floor, made sure I had my phone, and headed out to Keep Grounded to see if it was quiet enough for me to have another conversation with Tara.

Chapter Twelve

As soon as I walked in, I saw it was a totally different atmosphere from days ago. It was full of people when I came in—students, professionals having meetings, and more moms and toddlers. I was glad I had the ebook version of my book on my phone because I was definitely going to have to wait if I wanted the opportunity to speak quietly with Tara. I ordered my coffee and got a croissant, then lucked out by slipping into a small table that had been vacated just moments before.

The coffee shop was lively and pretty loud, but as soon as I started reading my book, it all disappeared. That was, perhaps, a gift bestowed on me from spending so much time in the library—the ability to block out the buzz around me and get my work knocked out. When I next looked up, there were just a few tables with people at them and things had gotten much quieter. Tara came over to chat.

"That was quite a rush," I said after greeting her. "You're really getting some good business in here."

"It comes and goes," she said with a laugh. "And it's totally unpredictable. Sometimes I have students in here who'll ask me when the best time to come in to study is and I really have no idea. It can get crazy in the mornings, but then it can sometimes get just as crazy in the afternoons." She added, "No work today?"

"It's my day off," I said with a smile.

"It looked like you were doing some reading," said Tara. "How's the book going . . . *House of Mirth*, wasn't it?"

"Oh, things are generally heading downhill for Lily Bart," I said lightly. "But it's not an unexpected development."

Tara said, "Hey, I wanted to thank you for the book recommendation list. I popped by the library during my lunch one day and grabbed one of them. But I haven't had a chance to read yet because I had a date."

I raised my eyebrows. "Really? Did it go well?"

Tara snorted. "It was a total disaster. Oh my gosh. I swear I'll *never* go on another blind date. They're always awful."

I chuckled. "Amen to that. I'll have to tell you sometime about some of the blind dates I've suffered through."

We chatted lightly for a few more minutes before I turned serious. "Actually, I kind of wanted to talk to you. Something else has happened. Have you heard?"

"No, and usually I'm one of the ones who hears all the gossip first. You don't mean that someone else has died?"

"I'm afraid so. Frank Morrison."

Tara's face grew grim. "I see. You know, I did have a fleeting moment in the middle of all the busyness where I realized he hadn't come in for his daily fix. I could usually set a clock by him. I was wondering if maybe he was sick." She shook her head. "Well, I hate to hear about anybody's death, although I do feel a little more conflicted about his than most. Considering what he might have been guilty of. What happened?"

I filled her in with what little I knew. "I'm just trying to talk it all through, mostly. I know you hear things around town and wondered if you'd heard anything about Frank. You know, in terms of his getting on people's bad sides."

Tara snorted. "You mean besides Ellie's? That's the thing that's surprising—I'd have thought Frank killed Ellie. But now I don't know what to think. Still, I'm sure there are other people he might have rubbed the wrong way. After all, his personality could be rough around the edges. He seemed kind of pushy and bossy. He's a good customer, but I have a hard time getting a word in edgewise because he interrupts me a lot. He seems pretty dismissive of women altogether, actually—except for Sunny Griffith, of course."

"Sunny? He had dealings with her?" This seemed very unlikely to me, at least from a personal standpoint.

Tara said quickly, "Oh, no, they weren't involved or anything. Can you imagine that? Those two would be hard to picture together."

"Well, I guess there are some odd-couples out there," I said.

"True. But not the two of them. No, they were both in the shop getting coffee recently and Sunny remembered Frank did work at the library. She asked if he also did 'for-hire' work for individuals. Frank told her he was an independent contractor and could work for anyone. Sunny asked him if he might be available to help with their home network. For her and Ted." Tara shrugged. "The only reason I thought the conversation was remarkable was that he didn't interrupt Sunny a single time. I've always thought he acted kind of dismissive around women. Still, I'm sorry to hear he's gone."

I took a sip of my coffee and said, "Hopefully the police will get to the bottom of it all soon."

"I hope so." The bell on the shop door rang and Tara smiled at me. "That's my cue. Better run. Hope you have a good day."

I glanced at the door to see who'd made it in and my heart skipped a beat as I saw a tired-looking Grayson walk in. He spotted me at once and gave a quick wave before ordering his coffee. Tara, apparently seeing something in my expression when Grayson entered the shop, gave me a wink.

He walked up to me a few minutes later with a large coffee. His hair and clothes were rumpled as if he'd slept in them and there were dark circles under his eyes. He hesitated before asking, "Are you waiting for somebody or can I join you?"

I gestured to the chair across from me and said, "Have a seat."

Grayson settled down and immediately took a long sip from the coffee. He grimaced at me and then gave me a rueful smile.

"Long night?" I asked. It was unusual seeing Grayson in such disarray. Ordinarily he was well put-together: more so than me, actually. Even when we went on hikes, he looked like someone modeling in an outdoor catalog.

"Unfortunately, it was. You might have heard by now—there was another murder here locally."

I said, "Oh, you were the newspaper reporter Burton was talking about. You were covering Frank Morrison's murder."

He nodded and gave a dry chuckle. "Sometimes I wonder if this town even really *needs* a newspaper. It seems to me that news travels pretty fast around here." He took another few gulps of his coffee, which must have burned his throat, considering how much steam was still coming off of it. He winced. "Just trying to wake up."

He was rapidly depleting the large coffee. After a few more gulps of the steaming coffee, he frowned and said, "Wait. I'm slow on the uptake today. You heard about Frank Morrison's death from *Burton* and not from local gossip?"

I nodded. "Frank did contract tech work for the library. Burton was just trying to get a picture of what Frank was like, I think."

Grayson said, "This is off the record, of course, but I'm a little curious what he was like, myself. It seemed like no one reported him missing, but I got the impression from Burton that he probably hadn't died right before the fisherman found him this morning. It sort of begs the question: what was he doing out there? Why was he at the lake in the dark?"

"I don't have a ton of insight to add on anything to do with Frank, unfortunately." Despite being off the record, I didn't feel totally comfortable sharing what I'd heard about Frank's treatment of his wife. It was one thing telling Burton and Wilson and something very different telling the editor of the local newspaper, as attractive as I might find him. "What I know about him was from work. He was capable at his job and always got our desktops or printers or copiers back in working order. He was pretty nerdy in terms of what his hobbies were, I think."

Grayson said, "So Frank probably wasn't out at the lake getting exercise or something, then."

It was almost exactly what Burton had asked me. I shrugged. "I guess he *could* have been. Maybe he was trying to improve his health or something. But it seems like an odd time to be doing it. I don't think he was a fitness nut or anything."

"Speaking of fitness, I'm looking forward to our hike," said Grayson with a quick segue. We firmed up our plans for taking it and what food we'd bring for the picnic. Then he added, "It must be nice to catch up with old friends around town."

I smiled. "Everyone is always telling me I need to get out of the library more and I'm starting to finally take their words to heart." It was too early for me to talk about Connor, especially since I wasn't completely sure myself what sort of relationship we were embarking on.

"What was high school like here in Whitby?" he asked.

I considered this. "Well, I guess it's different for everyone, but I really had a good time. We all knew each other by that point. I liked my teachers and had a few great English teachers who influenced me in and outside the classroom—recommended books for me to read and that kind of thing. I had a small group of friends and we did a lot together . . . mostly outdoor stuff, which is why I know as much about the hiking trails here as I do."

"And you dated Connor back then, you said."

Connor again. "That's right. Mostly, again, it was just hanging out at the lake and going out on trails since neither of us had any money to do much else. We'd eat fast food if we ate out at all. There were even fewer food options at the time than there are now, as hard as that might be to believe. Sometimes we'd grab our own food from home and hang out at the park with our friends." I shrugged. "Typical high school stuff, I guess. Minus the school sports. Our teams weren't that hot."

Grayson looked wistful. "It sounds like fun, though. I wish I'd been in Whitby then."

"You didn't enjoy high school as much?"

He shook his head. "Nope. My family moved around a lot so I was always the new kid every time. I was in three different high schools."

I winced. "Those aren't great years to be moving. I'd think it would be tough to adjust when you don't even really have a handle on your own sense of self yet."

"Plus, I was super-quiet at the time and spent most of my time doing nerdy things, sort of like we were saying Frank did." He gave a rueful smile.

"Hey, there's nothing wrong with nerdy pursuits," I said quickly. "I'm kind of an expert in those, myself."

"Anyway, it would have been great to have grown up here. I've really enjoyed living in Whitby so far."

I said as casually as I could, "Do you have long-term plans for staying here? Or is this sort of a layover-type job? I know, from a journalism standpoint, that sometimes being willing to move can open more opportunities."

Grayson laughed and I felt that happy heart-bounce that I always did when he laughed. "I'm planning on staying put. After spending the first half of my life moving around practically every year, the idea of putting down roots in a place is really appealing. I mean, you're right—if I were more ambitious, I should be open to getting calls about editor openings from other, bigger newspapers. But I just can't seem to get interested in doing that." He paused. "But here I am, still the new guy in town."

"Yeah, but it's not like you're not out and about in town all the time. Being on the newspaper has got to mean that you're meeting people every day."

Grayson said, "That's true, but I'm not really getting acquainted with them and it's always on more of a professional level. I don't feel like I'm putting myself out there and making friends." He mulled this for a moment or two. "Maybe I need to get involved in some different things. Maybe I should be on the HOA board after all, as a way to get to know people."

"I don't think you're *that* desperate."

He grinned at me. "Maybe not." He paused and said offhandedly, "I probably just need to try to develop the friendships I already have. Would you like to grab supper sometime? I mean, just after work or something. You mentioned you were trying to get out more, too."

I felt a flush rise up from my neck and mentally scolded myself. The guy was trying to make real friends. As pretty much the only staff for the local paper, he was working all the time. It didn't really mean anything. I said as breezily as I could manage, "Sure, Grayson. That would be great."

He smiled. "Awesome."

I glanced at my watch. "I guess I should be heading out. You've inspired me to do better with my exercise and I told myself I was going to go to the park after this. Are you going to try to get some sleep?"

He snorted. "Not after that huge cup of coffee." He looked at me, considering. "Would you mind company? For the exercise, I mean. I could meet you over at the park. It looks like it's going to rain later, so it would be better for me to exercise this morning."

My heart skipped. "Sure, we'll meet up at the park so we can change first." I glanced at my watch. "Maybe in forty-five minutes?"

"See you then."

Forty-five minutes later I drove into a parking spot at the park. The weather might be going downhill that afternoon, but it was perfect for now. There was a light breeze as I stepped out of the car and a few clouds kept the sun from being too unbearable. The park was one of my favorite places to go. There were wide trails through the trees that connected to the greenway we had around town. There was a big pond—or maybe a small lake—in the center of the park and several people walking their dogs and pushing babies in strollers while getting views of the mountains in the background.

Grayson drove up and hopped out of the car. He was wearing some serious-looking athletic clothes and I glanced down at my own baggy tee shirt and old shorts.

"You look like you're ready to run," I said in a slightly accusatory voice.

Grayson looked abashed. "We weren't going to run?"

I said with a smile, "I'll either need to jog slowly or do a really fast walk."

"That's all I'm really up for anyway. After all, I didn't get any sleep last night. I just put this stuff on out of habit."

"At least you *have* an exercise habit. I'm also going to need to stretch for a few minutes," I said ruefully.

We were stretching when I noticed a familiar couple walking toward us down the trail. Ted noticed me at exactly the same time and I immediately got the impression he wanted to avoid me. After all, he had to know I suspected his involvement with Ellie wasn't solely due to Spanish lessons. Sunny, on the other hand, gave me a quick wave and came right on over, professional as always.

I remembered Grayson saying how he still felt like the new kid in Whitby, and he didn't seem to know either of the Griffiths. I quickly introduced them. Ted, still acting eager to avoid me, delved into conversation with Grayson, asking how the small, local newspaper was doing financially.

Sunny said in a friendly voice, "You were serious about getting more exercise! You know, we did get some really cute athletic clothes in at Nearly New recently. You should come by and take a look."

I glanced down again at my clothes. "That might not be a bad idea. These are fine for exercising, but I was just looking at what Grayson had on and realized I might end up really hot if we go for a run. I need to get something more breathable. For some reason, despite the small amount of fabric, athletic clothing is ridiculously expensive."

Sunny said in a much more solemn tone, "On a completely different matter, I hear violent death has impacted the library again. Is that true?" She pursed her lips.

Fortunately, Ted joined us again right then. This was good because I wasn't really sure how to answer that question. Was it an indictment of the library's hiring practices?

Ted said, "Violent death hasn't impacted the library *directly*, dear."

I could sense an underlying current of tension between Ted and Sunny, but it looked to me as if they were definitely trying to make things work. If Sunny did know about Ted's affair with Ellie, it sure seemed to me as if she was trying to move forward and past it. They were exercising together. They were attending funerals together. At any rate, it looked like they were both putting some effort into their marriage.

Grayson was looking interested, probably from a professional aspect, at the mention of Frank's death.

I said, "You're talking about Frank Morrison. He did a good deal of technology and electronics work for us at the library whenever something went wrong."

"Do a lot of things go wrong?" asked Sunny with a frown.

"Well, he was over at the library every couple of weeks if not more," I said with a small laugh. "A lot of the time it was the copier he was working on. You know, when you have the public trying to figure out a copier, you get mixed results. And, sometimes, a broken copier. But he also worked on our printer, the desktops, and other things for us." I paused. "He also did contract work for individuals, I believe. Didn't he do some work at your house?"

I waited to see if either one of them would take the bait. Tara had sounded pretty positive that Frank had helped Sunny and Ted with their network.

Ted interjected, "Sure, he did, remember, Sunny? He helped us with some network problems we were having. Our laptops weren't talking to our printer and we'd have to plug them in to the printer and print manually. He helped us with some other stuff, too."

Sunny's expression looked a bit cold. Although, it was hard to really tell since she frequently had a fairly static expression on her face that I suspected might be owed to Botox injections. "I don't remember discussing Frank's work with you, Ann." There was a slight chill in her voice.

Grayson raised his eyebrows and looked even more interested.

I quickly said, "Oh, I think it's something Frank mentioned when I was speaking with him one time."

"It seems an odd thing for him to mention," said Sunny.

I shrugged. "He probably knew of your connection with the library and figured I'd know you."

Sunny said, "Did you hear much about what happened to Frank? We've only heard the basics."

I gestured over to Grayson. "He's probably the guy to ask. He was on the scene, reporting. And didn't get much sleep."

"We'll have a full story in the paper tomorrow," said Grayson. "But the gist of it is that a fisherman discovered Frank's body in the lake early this morning. They're investigating it, but it seems it was murder."

Sunny sighed.

"I guess you must have gotten to know Frank pretty well? With him working in your home, I mean," said Grayson.

Sunny quickly said, "I don't think we'd say we knew him *well*." She looked at her husband. "Still, dear, you thought he had something of a temper, didn't you?"

"Did I?" asked Ted, looking surprised.

"Don't you remember? You said something about him getting upset when he was working on our network."

Ted said, "Oh, that. Well, that was nothing. Computers are very annoying things, aren't they? Something wasn't working correctly, and he was letting a little off-color language fly before I walked into the room. He stopped as soon as I'd come in. I'd probably have done the same."

Grayson said to Sunny, "So you're thinking maybe Frank had a temper and made somebody angry? Got on someone's bad side?"

Sunny shrugged. "I don't know what I think. I'm just trying to work it out so it all makes sense in my head. At any rate, Ann, these are two deaths connected, however tenuously, to the library. I know sometimes you work late shifts, don't you?"

"Frequently, yes. I work one tomorrow night."

Sunny said, "I just want to make sure you're taking care of yourself. Maybe you should wear a whistle or carry some pepper spray? Or maybe use one of those apps when you walk to your car—you know, the kinds that if you take your finger off your phone, they automatically call the police for you."

She wasn't wrong, but somehow in my gut I didn't really think someone was just randomly attacking library employees and contract workers. But I said, "That's a good idea, Sunny. Thank you."

"Well, we should let you go exercise now," said Sunny, and Ted looked relieved. "Good to see you, Ann, and good to meet you, Grayson."

Chapter Thirteen

We started a fast walk on the trail leading around the small lake and Grayson said, "You know, I wouldn't have put those two together as a couple."

"They make a nice-*looking* couple," I said mildly.

"They do. It's just that their personalities don't seem to mesh that well. Sunny seems very reserved and a little icy. Ted is warmer and a bit more outgoing. At least, that's how they appear, anyway."

I said, "Well, people say opposites attract." I would have liked to have talked with Grayson more about the complexities of Ted and Sunny's marriage and Ellie's involvement with it, but hesitated because of Grayson's job. Not that I thought Grayson would print pure gossip in the newspaper . . . that would basically amount to slander.

Grayson glanced over at me perceptively. "There's something more there, isn't there?" He paused. "I know it could be hard to share information with me because of my working on the paper, but I promise anything you tell me is totally off the record and wouldn't go any further."

I hesitated another few moments and said slowly, "Honestly, I'd like these murders solved. Maybe if you're thinking over these bits and pieces and Burton is thinking them over and *I'm* thinking them over, we might get somewhere faster. But Grayson, I'm not sure there's anything really here that will help get to the bottom of it all."

I filled him in on what little I knew about Ted and Ellie's relationship—how he'd claimed he was giving her Spanish lessons but how their involvement seemed a lot more than simply educational. I talked about Ellie's and Sunny's awkward run-ins in the library and I wondered if perhaps Ellie had tried to put pressure on Sunny to end her marriage.

Grayson was a great listener. He nodded his head, paying close attention to what I was saying. Then he said, "It definitely sounds like a possibility. I'll keep my ears open too and see what I find out."

Then he switched to other, lighter topics as we quickly walked around the trail. I asked him more about the different places he'd lived growing up and he chatted about that and his impressions of Whitby so far and, before I knew it, the walk was over.

I grinned at him. "Did you wear enough of that coffee off that maybe you can catch some sleep?"

He laughed. "Maybe. I'm going to try, anyway. There's no way I'll be able to come up with tomorrow's edition unless I get some kind of a nap in." He paused. "Hey, I enjoyed this. Thanks for letting me tag along."

"My pleasure," I said, still feeling that little zing of energy when he looked in my eyes.

The rest of my day off was spent in what I'd call "deliberately unproductive mode." I'm usually trying to strike things off my list, even when I'm at home, but sometimes it's good to really just unplug as much as possible. I sent a couple of emails, but then settled down with Fitz on the sofa. He curled up into me and I curled up into him and I read my book and then watched a British detective show on TV and petted Fitz as he purred loudly.

It was a good thing I'd gotten in some relaxation time because the next day at work was pretty nonstop all the way until closing time. I ushered out the last couple of patrons, both of whom seemed reluctant to go, nine o'clock or not.

I was heading for my older-model Subaru when a man suddenly started walking toward me.

I drew my breath in as a startled hiss and positioned my laptop bag so I could swing it at him if I needed to.

The man stopped and then apologetically said, "Ann. Sorry, I must have startled you. It's Ted. Ted Griffith."

He stepped under one of the streetlights and I saw it was him. I relaxed my shoulders a little, feeling some of the tension drain out of them, although I was still on alert, wondering what he was doing in the library parking lot after hours, especially in light of current events.

I pressed my lips together tightly. "Ted. I didn't expect to see you out here. We just closed the library for the night."

I hadn't really thought he was here to use the library, especially since I hadn't noticed him being much of a regular patron in the past.

He shook his head. "I'm not here to visit the library. I'm here to see you."

I positioned myself so I could swiftly pivot and make it into my car. "Okay. The problem is that it's been a really long day. I was planning on just going home and climbing into bed before I have to do this all over again tomorrow. Can we talk another time?"

Ted's face was apologetic, but he seemed determined. "Look, I'm sorry I startled you. It's just that I wanted to have a conversation in private and I thought this was the best way to do it."

I set Fitz's carrier on the ground but kept my heavy laptop bag on my shoulder just in case. "Okay," I said cautiously.

Ted looked flustered. "It's just that I keep running into you when I'm out with Sunny and I know you've figured out that Ellie and I were . . . you know."

"Having a relationship?" I asked archly.

"Exactly," he said, looking relieved that he didn't have to spell it out. "I feel bad about it, but the fact is I didn't have *anything* to do with Ellie's death. I made a mistake and now what I want to do is to make it up with my wife. I love Sunny and I'll do anything to make sure we make our marriage work."

"Okay," I repeated slowly. "What does this have to do with me?"

Ted said in a rush, "I don't want Sunny to find out about Ellie and me. There's absolutely no reason for her to know about it, especially with Ellie being gone. I want to make sure you're not going to say anything to her about it. It seems like you two are becoming friendly."

That was a stretch. Being friendly and becoming friends were two entirely different things. I said, "She doesn't know?"

Ted paled a little. "Not at all. Don't even suggest that she knows."

As far as I could tell, Sunny might know a lot more than Ted thought she did. But if he was being genuine, and he certainly seemed to be, he wanted to make sure she didn't know anything about it because he thought she didn't have a clue—and he wanted to remain in the marriage.

"Okay," I said slowly. I paused. "Did Ellie try to pressure you into leaving Sunny?"

He nodded his head. "Yes. But I would never have hurt Ellie, Ann, you have to believe that. But yeah, it was really a worry of mine. Ellie was convinced she and I could have a relationship together. She'd told me she was going to tell Sunny so Sunny would leave me and we could get married."

"How did you react to that?" I asked.

He made a face. "Not well. I feel bad about that now because she's gone. I did a lot of yelling, mostly because I felt like I wasn't getting through to her at all. Ellie had a plan, and she wasn't going to let anything stand in the way of it. She wouldn't accept I didn't feel the same way she did. In her head, we could have this perfect life together as soon as Sunny was out of the picture."

I said, "You don't think she told Sunny about your relationship?"

Once again, Ted's face was pale and grim at the suggestion. "No. Sunny hasn't said a word to me about it. Ellie did threaten to tell Sunny if I didn't."

I wondered if Sunny had felt as protective over her marriage to Ted as Ellie had with her relationship with Ted. Maybe something in my expression conveyed this to Ted because he said quickly, "I don't think for a minute that Sunny would have murdered Ellie."

"Not even if she suddenly confronted Sunny about it? Could she have asked Ellie to meet her at the library to talk in private and then Sunny lashed out at her?"

Ted was shaking his head the entire time I was speaking. "No. I don't believe it. Sunny would never do that. You've seen her—she's totally contained."

"Even if her marriage was being threatened?"

Ted said, "Anyway, Sunny was with me. She couldn't have been at the library when Ellie was killed."

But his flush was a giveaway. Maybe he and Sunny were each other's alibis because they were both out that night and were not only protecting each other, but themselves.

"Frank's death—do you think it could have anything to do with Ellie's?" asked Ted.

"I have no idea. Although it does seem unusual that there would be two unrelated deaths in Whitby. Do you think they're connected?"

Ted nodded, looking as if he was latching onto the idea. "Yes. I mean, we talked about it yesterday at the park, right? By the way, Grayson seemed like a nice guy."

I was grateful for the cloak of darkness as I felt my face turn red. "He is nice. We're friends—actually, he's a neighbor of mine."

Ted nodded absently and then said, "Like I said, when we were talking about Frank at the park yesterday, at first I didn't really picture Frank being involved in Ellie's death. But now it's not seeming as random as I thought. He *did* have a temper. He was working in the library a lot with computer repairs, right?"

"Not really a *lot*, but he was regularly in there."

Ted continued, "Maybe he was interested in Ellie. Why not? He was a widower and Ellie was single. He could have asked her out and been rejected. Maybe he was angry or frustrated or something and took it out on Ellie."

I wasn't going to get into Ellie's blackmailing activities with Frank, so I said cautiously, "Sure. That could have happened."

This validation made Ted straighten up. "That's what I'm thinking. I'm going to tell the cops my theory the next time I see them."

"Have they been speaking with you?" I asked, trying to sound nonchalant. "I mean, it seems they're trying to cast a wide net to figure out what happened."

Ted ran a nervous hand through his hair. "Yeah. They've come twice to the office to talk to me. I'm worried sick they're going to come to my house to ask me questions and tip off Sunny."

"They're asking about your relationship with Ellie?"

"They know. Maybe they guessed or they didn't believe me when I said I was giving Ellie Spanish lessons. But that's why I've come to talk to you. I really need you to keep this quiet, Ann."

Ted reached out and clutched my arm, rougher than he should have and I winced.

Right then a car pulled into the parking lot with its high-beam headlights were turned on, blinding us. Ted released my arm and backed up, blinking. "What the heck?"

The car pulled right up next to us and I saw it was a police cruiser. Burton rolled down his window and said in a clipped voice, "Everything all right here, Ann?"

"Yeah," I said, rubbing my arm where Ted had grabbed it. "Everything's okay. I'm just wanting to get back home with Fitz, though. Long day."

Burton nodded briskly. "Sounds good. I'll watch while you get in your car."

As I picked up Fitz's cat carrier and fumbled with my keys, I could hear Burton say in an icy tone to Ted, "What were you thinking?"

Ted sounded sullen. "I was just talking to Ann."

"It sure didn't look that way to me. It's after-hours at the library. We've already had one death here in the past week and I want to make sure there's no more trouble. Is that understood?"

Ted muttered something and Burton said, "Good. If you have library-related business, you come during library hours."

Ted hurried into his car and took off.

"Everything okay, Ann?" Burton asked me again.

I sighed. "Ted suspects I know about him and Ellie. He was trying to make sure I didn't say anything to Sunny about it. He thinks Sunny doesn't have a clue."

Burton snorted. "I think it's *Ted* who doesn't have a clue." He reached over to the passenger seat and said, "Here. This is the reason I came by tonight."

I took a small paper bag from him and looked inside. There were a couple of pepper spray bottles inside.

He said gruffly, "Just thought it wouldn't hurt for you and Luna to carry some, especially considering there's been a violent crime here and because y'all frequently are locking up late."

I gave him a warm smile. "Thanks, Burton. You're right—with everything going on right now, it sure won't hurt to carry some pepper spray on us. I'll give one of them to Luna tomorrow."

He gave a cheerful wave and watched as I climbed into my Subaru and started off for home.

The next couple of days passed fairly quietly. Because the library wasn't as busy as usual, I was able to knock out some work I hadn't been able to get around to—graphics for our social media pages (most of them, naturally, featuring endearing pictures of Fitz), displays of similarly-themed books for patrons to browse through, and my Ask Fitz advice column.

I also had another date with Connor. This time he picked me up from my house and brought me flowers.

"That's so sweet of you," I stuttered, pawing through the backs of my kitchen cabinets to try and find a vase of some description. Besides prom, I'd never gotten a bouquet of flowers before and it flustered me.

It also flustered me that Connor had gotten all dressed up for our date and I hadn't realized we were going somewhere fancy.

I glanced down at my cotton top and black slacks and said, "Hey, I'm just going to change real quick."

Connor put his hands up. "No, no," he said. "Don't worry about it. Let's just go grab something to eat."

I still felt uncomfortable. Here he was in a suit, minus the jacket, and I looked like I was dressed for a trip to the deli. Actually, I *was* dressed for a trip to the deli. I could have sworn he'd told me last time that we'd go there because he wanted to try out the chicken salad wrap I'd told him was so good. "No, I'll feel better if I change. For some reason, I had it stuck in my head that we were going to the deli tonight."

"Maybe we'll go there for lunch soon," he said.

This time he didn't try and stop me, so I headed to the back to pull on a simple black cotton dress, which I dressed up a little with some of the jewelry I'd gotten at the consignment shop. At this rate, I was definitely going to have to go back there and load up on dressier clothes. I told myself Connor was being nice to take me somewhere swankier, but part of me was irritated he hadn't told me in advance. Maybe he was the kind of guy who liked surprises, like the flowers. But somehow, it rubbed me the wrong way. Probably because I'd never liked being caught off-guard. That was one reason I was such a planner.

I was finished getting ready in just a couple of minutes. But then I got a text message from Luna. *I'm doing a little detecting, haha. Trudy, who I know as a mom from storytime, works with Connor. Just FYI, she mentioned to me she'd seen Connor really screw something up a couple of weeks ago at the hospital, although he thought no one had noticed. Maybe good he's not your main squeeze, since Trudy was thinking about reporting him. Trudy also used to talk to Ellie here at the library!*

I wrote Luna back to compliment her sleuthing, although I wasn't sure she really had anything there. It wasn't good to mess up at the hospital, for sure. But even if Trudy had mentioned Connor's error to Ellie, it didn't mean Connor had murdered Ellie to keep her quiet. After all, I'd known Connor most of my life. He liked *saving* lives, not taking them. I walked back out to the living room.

"You look great," said Connor with a grin.

At least I felt a little more comfortable with how I looked, but I still felt like I'd been thrown off a bit . . . both by having to change and Luna's unsettling text. "Ready to go?" I asked lightly.

Connor did a good job of putting me back at ease on the drive to the restaurant. At least, he did before I noticed we were driving out of Whitby. "We're heading out of town?" I asked, interrupting Connor. Maybe I needed to learn how to relax, but I was starting to feel like my evening was being hijacked.

"Oh, there's a new place in Asheville a friend told me about. I thought maybe we could check it out. Is that okay with you?"

His last sentence sounded more like a rhetorical question and so I shrugged and said, "Sure," as Connor continued telling a story about something that had happened at work. I gritted my teeth as I pretended to listen. I was tired from my day at the library and now I was tired and irritated. At least there was the promise of what sounded like a good meal at the end of the drive. And, at the speed Connor was driving, it seemed like we were going to get there sooner rather than later.

The sky had been alternating all day between looking threatening and glaring sunlight. This had apparently made the air unstable, kicking off a tremendous storm. We drove right into it and I was glad to see Connor hit the brakes at least a little bit. He turned up his wipers as fast as they could go and seemed to be paying more attention to the road, which was a relief.

Then he gave me a sideways look. "I was talking to my uncle on the phone earlier. He was saying that Ellie's death, in addition to being upsetting for everyone at the library, was also a hardship in terms of staff. He was implying you might be more tired than you usually are."

I hid a smile at this. Wilson was obviously still not sold on my dating Connor. Again, though, I found it kind of touching instead of annoying. It was nice to latch onto a good reason for my general quietness and resistance to going out on a date to begin with.

"I knew Ellie, just very briefly," said Connor casually.

I stiffened. He hadn't mentioned this before and surely he'd known about Ellie's death, although I hadn't mentioned it to him.

"I know she was a coworker of yours, but were the two of you friendly? I'd imagine it's been hard, emotionally, on you if you were."

I turned to study his profile but his expression was unreadable as he stared straight ahead through the windshield. "Ellie was still new at the library, so we really didn't know each other very well. It was still a real shock of course, though." I hesitated and then added, still trying to get a read on Connor, "Plus, from what I've learned recently, Ellie had an unfortunate predilection for blackmail so she might not have been great friend material."

His face was still inscrutable. "I didn't realize that," he said finally.

I shifted uneasily in the passenger seat and looked out the window at the coursing rain as he sped up again. "You never mentioned where we're eating tonight," I said in a rather forced, light tone.

He chuckled, still looking directly ahead and still pressing hard on the accelerator. "Somewhere where we won't be seen by anyone we know. I remember how small towns are."

My breathing accelerated and my heart pounded hard in my chest. "I hate to bring this up, Connor, but I'm actually not feeling very well. Maybe it would be best if I went back home. I'm sorry."

This finally got a reaction from Connor as he swung his head around to look at me in surprise.

Suddenly, as he took his attention off the road, he hit a puddle. More, actually, a small pond of water right on the highway. His car hydroplaned, skidding off the road as Connor struggled to control it.

Chapter Fourteen

I clutched onto the armrest, holding my breath as we hit a ditch and the car came to a crashing stop.

"Are you okay?" asked Connor, staring at me with wide eyes.

I nodded. "I think so. Are you?"

"Yeah," he said absently. He frowned. "I'm going to see what kind of damage there is."

It was still pouring down rain. "Do you have an umbrella or something in here?"

Connor shook his head. "It's okay."

He stepped out and peered at the car, swiping impatiently at his face as the wind buffeted rain at him. Then he got back into the car.

He looked relieved. "I can't really see any damage. Let me see if I can drive us out of the ditch."

Connor stepped on the accelerator and the engine revved but the car didn't move. He turned the steering wheel a different way and tried again, but it just didn't budge. This was one of those situations where we'd be better off in my old Subaru with the all-wheel drive than in his expensive sedan.

I really didn't want to get out of the car. It had been a long day and the weather was pretty unrelenting. But I also didn't want to be stuck in this ditch. I reluctantly said, "Should I get out of the car? Maybe if the weight is redistributed then you can get it to move."

Connor gave me an apologetic grimace. "Would you mind? It's worth a try. Sorry—I know you're not feeling well."

I hopped out and into the gale. Connor pressed on the accelerator again and I watched as the wheels spun but didn't get any traction to move the car. Whether Connor wanted to face it or not, it was obvious to me that the vehicle was going to need to be towed out of the ditch.

He motioned me back in the car and I happily climbed back in, wishing I had a towel or something as rivulets of rain coursed down me. Even though it was a warm day, I shivered.

Connor had apparently finally reached the same conclusion I had. "Guess I'm going to need to call for a tow." He sighed as he pulled his phone out of his pocket. He gave me an apologetic smile. "Apparently, the universe is trying to tell us that this isn't a great night for our date. Should we take a rain check?"

I was relieved. "Of course we can." I hadn't wanted to go out in the first place and then I'd gotten weirded out by Connor talking about Ellie.

He was on the phone with the garage when a car pulled up to see if we were all right. I couldn't see inside the car because of the torrential rain until the driver lowered his window. I grinned when I saw my favorite patron Linus there. In his copilot seat was his dog Ivy, looking very interested in the proceedings.

Linus's eyebrows were drawn together in concern. "Is everybody okay?"

"We're fine, but the car is disabled, so my friend is calling for a tow," I said.

"I could give you a ride back home, if you wanted," he said.

I hesitated. I had the feeling Connor was going to want to speak with the tow truck driver and I didn't want to totally desert him. Although, truth be told, it was extremely tempting.

Connor put his hand over his phone and said, "Hey, Ann, if you want to head out, that's okay. I wouldn't want you to have to wait for the tow driver with me."

I said slowly, "Okay. Then I could head back out and pick you up in my car when you're done." It was, honestly, the last thing in the world I wanted to do, but I figured an offer needed to be made.

He shook his head. "Nope. I'm not going to have you drive back out in this mess. No need for *both* of us to wreck our cars. I'll just call an uber once I've gotten everything settled. No worries, okay?"

Again, I felt nothing but a huge sense of relief. I couldn't help but think if I'd been with Grayson, I might have felt differently. Plus, I really couldn't picture Grayson speeding like that in weather like this. "Okay. Thanks, Connor. Be careful, okay?"

I carefully climbed back out of Connor's car and hopped into Linus's backseat.

He turned and said apologetically, "I'd have you sit in the front seat with me, but Ivy's fur would get all over you."

"Linus, I'm just sorry I'm soaking your back seat with water. Thank you so much for getting me out of there."

His gentle features were concerned. "I'm just glad I happened to be coming back from a trip to the dog park. Are you sure you're okay? That must have been quite a jolt you took."

For the first time, I glanced back at Connor's car in the ditch. From the road, I could really tell exactly how big that ditch was and what a crazy angle the car was stuck at. We hadn't had a chance of getting that vehicle out of there; I could see that now.

"You know, I think it just scared me more than hurt me. The whole thing seemed to happen in slow motion."

Linus seemed satisfied that he didn't need to drive me for medical attention. He turned back around and put his car in gear and said firmly, "Well, Ivy and I are going to get you back home to Fitz now. Enough of being out in this storm."

It was rather nice to be fussed over. As Linus set out slowly down the road, windshield wipers flapping furiously, I leaned back on the seat and felt some of the stress drain out of me.

Linus gripped the steering wheel tightly with both hands as he sat on the edge of the seat and navigated through the storm. He said, "I hope things settle down for you soon, Ann. You've really gone through a lot of stress lately, what with Ellie's death."

I gave a short laugh. "You'd think the life of a librarian wouldn't be very exciting, wouldn't you?"

He said in his careful way, "Have you heard if there are any more developments in Ellie's case?"

I blew out a breath. "If anything, it's gotten more complicated. One of the guys who fixes computers and other electronics for us has been murdered. There might have been a connection with Ellie. Of course, as you mentioned yourself, Ellie seemed to be capable of blackmail. There's no telling right now what might have happened to her."

Ivy turned around to give me a sad, soulful look in response to my tone.

Linus said a bit uncomfortably, "I did see Ellie getting out of a man's car a few times when I was returning to the library after lunch. I wonder now if she might have been involved with someone. And if he ended up doing her harm."

Linus was always so quiet that it was easy to forget how much he was taking in all the time. "You're very observant. Yes, the police are aware of a relationship she was having. It sounds like that's another possibility for them to investigate."

Linus had the heater on which, under ordinary circumstances in a North Carolina summer, would be absolutely unbearable. But because of the fact I was soaked through and had had a pretty frightening experience, it was soothing. Ivy, who was definitely not soaked, looked rather warm as her tongue lolled out. She smiled a doggy smile at me from the front seat, which felt very reassuring. Linus had instrumental jazz music playing softly in the background and the combination of all the ingredients made me start feeling sleepy.

Since I could easily envision myself falling asleep and engaging in noisy snoring, I kept the conversation going so I could stay awake. "I was lucky you and Ivy came by. Otherwise, I'd probably have been stuck there in a really weird angle in that car for a while."

Linus's face was concerned again in the rear-view mirror. "Yes, like I mentioned, Ivy and I had gone to the dog park in Asheville for a while. Then I got a weather alert on my phone, so we packed up and started back right when the storm started up." He paused, seeming to struggle between his concern and his respect for privacy. "Was everything all right? I mean, with you and that young man? It was a hydroplaning event, I suppose?"

"Well, it was certainly a hydroplane. I wonder if it would have happened if we hadn't been going so fast and he hadn't been distracted," I said a bit sourly. Then I quickly added, "Sorry, that's just me being tired. Connor is a nice guy."

"Is he?" asked Linus. I couldn't fault him for the question since his only experience around him was when Connor had driven his vehicle into a ditch.

"Absolutely," I said with perhaps more enthusiasm than I actually felt. "We grew up together here. Went to school together."

Linus nodded quickly, always eager to agree. But his kind face was still a little worried and I had to admit it was nice to be fretted over, even though I thought his concern was misplaced.

As Linus dropped me off, I hurried inside since there were still buckets of rain coming down. He waited until I got safely in the door and waved from inside the house and he cautiously backed out of my driveway.

Fitz hurried up to rub lovingly against me, but quickly backed away when he realized how sopping wet I was. "I know, buddy," I said ruefully. "I'm going to take care of that now."

Of course, to Fitz's astonishment, the way I chose to take care of it was to climb into a hot bath. I could tell by the expression on his furry face that he didn't comprehend how getting even wetter was going to help my situation. But it definitely did. I'd grabbed my book and a glass of wine and even lit myself a candle and tossed some bubble bath stuff into the tub as it ran.

Fitz kept an eye on me from a safe distance as he settled on the bathmat, tail curled around him.

The bath apparently did the trick because I was soothed enough to fall quickly asleep—even without eating supper. I guess all the stress from the day had really knocked me out. Fitz had snuggled up with me and we both slept hard until the alarm went off the next morning. It was a good thing I wasn't on the schedule to open up because for once I was still groggy, dragging, and running a little behind.

When I arrived at the library a few minutes after opening, Linus was already there, as usual, in his suit. He gave me a warm smile and a quick wave from the periodicals section where he was collecting the first of several morning newspapers to read.

Wilson spotted me and motioned to me to step into his office for a moment. I frowned, wondering if the fact that I was seven minutes behind schedule for once in my career was the cause for this impromptu meeting.

But when I walked in, Wilson was giving me a worried look. "My sister called me last night and told me about Connor's crash. Are you all right? Do you need a day off today?"

Mona definitely seemed to have created a kinder and gentler version of Wilson than the stern taskmaster I'd seen in the past. "Thanks, Wilson, I appreciate that. But I'm absolutely fine. I was just a little shaken up last night and pretty exhausted from the experience. All completely fixed, though, with a good night's sleep."

Wilson frowned and said rather sharply, "Was he driving too fast? The weather was atrocious last night. My sister said he was driving out of town."

"He'd made dinner reservations in Asheville. He was being thoughtful."

Wilson grumbled, "It seems as if he could have been thoughtful on a night with better weather."

"All's well that ends well. Did you hear who my gallant rescuer was?"

"Not Connor apparently." Wilson's tone was still cranky.

"Linus."

Wilson frowned in confusion.

"Linus—the suited gentleman who's in our periodical section much of the day."

"Oh, right, right. Yes, he's been something of a fixture for years—a very *quiet* fixture. I always say good morning to him and he to me but he doesn't ever seem to want to engage in conversation. Honestly, his perpetual attendance here makes him blend right into the background. But you're saying he *rescued* you?"

I nodded. "In a manner of speaking. He arrived out of the blue . . . well, I guess out of the *gray* would be more appropriate . . . and took me back in the middle of the storm. Connor needed to stick around with the car and wait for the tow truck driver. Linus had Ivy in the car."

Wilson looked blankly at me.

"You remember the stray dog we had here at the library a while back?"

"He adopted her?" asked Wilson.

I nodded again.

"Well, it sounds as if he's a hero all round," said Wilson slowly. Then, this matter apparently settled to his satisfaction, he cleared his throat and said, "So, what's on the agenda for the library today?"

I filled Wilson in as to my plans for the day, which included a bunch of social media posts for the library and the tech drop-in that was going on later. There was a light tap on the office door as I was wrapping up and I turned to see Mona standing there, giving us a smile.

Wilson smiled back and motioned her in. Mona bustled in, holding a tote bag full of knitting supplies. "Thought I'd hang out here today," she said, giving Wilson a quick hug.

He blushed and started blustering and I hid a smile.

"I did a little baking this morning and have muffins in the breakroom," she said.

"Muffins?" My stomach growled. Part of my oversleeping meant that I'd only grabbed a yogurt before heading out of the house this morning. And, of course, I'd missed supper the night before.

"They're still warm," said Mona persuasively.

"Wow, you must have gotten up super-early this morning," I said.

"She's always very thoughtful," said Wilson gruffly.

Fitz came in through the office door to find me. He wound himself around my legs.

"Fitz thinks it's time for me to get to work," I said with a smile. "I'm going to grab a warm muffin and get to it."

Wilson's phone rang and Mona said ruefully, "That's my cue to start my knitting in the periodical section."

"Linus is already there to keep you company," I said.

Mona chuckled. "He's too quiet to be very much company. But he's become at least a little more sociable. He's been interested in what I'm knitting, I think. I keep seeing him stealing glances at it."

The morning progressed. Luna had a couple of back-to-back children's storytimes, so was switching gears from toddlers to preschoolers in the breaks between them. Fitz was so alert and playful that I was able to take a number of pictures of him to liven up our social media. Then I set up graphics to advertise some of the library's upcoming events.

Luna came up to the circulation desk after her second storytime was finished. "Whew. I don't know what I was thinking scheduling those two particular groups back to back."

"I thought you had a set schedule for the storytimes."

"I do, but some other group needed the community room during one of the usual times, so I had to make a change."

I said, "Hey, before I forget, Burton gave me something to give to you. He gave me one, too." I reached into my purse and pulled out one of the pepper sprays and said, "Want me to stick it in your purse? This purple one is yours, right?"

Luna nodded. "Wow. That's actually really nice of him to do. He drove my mom and me when we had the car trouble, too." She paused, mulling this over. Then, after a pause, she said, "What do you think of Burton?"

"Me? I think he's a fantastic guy. The reason I have those pepper sprays from him is because he drove by the library last night to check up on whoever was closing the library up and make sure we got to our car all right. And you know what? I really appreciated that because Ted was outside and just about scared me to death last night."

"What? What was he doing out there?"

I said, "He was trying to convince me not to mention to Sunny that he'd had an affair with Ellie."

"What a jerk," said Luna. "Why would he think you'd do that anyway?"

"He apparently thinks Sunny and I are becoming friends," I said with a chuckle. "It's more like I keep running into Sunny. But anytime I do, Ted becomes increasingly uncomfortable."

"Good! He deserves it. So he was hanging out . . . what? In the dark last night, waiting for you to come out of the library? That's super-creepy."

I shrugged. "I guess he wanted to see who was closing up the library. It could have been you and then he just would have driven off. But I don't think he realized exactly how creepy he was being until Burton drove up and got all stern with him and made him leave."

"Good for Burton," said Luna warmly. "So you think he's a great guy."

"He's the best. But I think it's more important what *you* think of him."

Luna said slowly, "I don't know. I wouldn't have thought he was my type at all. He's all law-and-order, you know."

I snorted. "I don't know if that's true. That's just his job. He doesn't come across as super tight-laced to me."

"Fair enough. Oh, I don't know. He's just been so nice lately. He's so gentle with my mom and she thinks he's such a gentleman. He even offered to help take a look at the car on his day off. He's a great listener. It's hard to find a man who is."

Luna almost sounded as if she was trying to convince me . . . or herself? . . . of Burton's attributes.

"Do you think . . . well, do you think Burton is into me at all, though?" asked Luna, a little furrow appearing between her brows.

I burst out laughing and Luna put her hands on her hips. She said, mock-crossly, "What's so funny."

"It's just that you're always so proud of your intuition and insight but you've been completely blind about Burton. For so long."

Luna colored a little and her eyes widened. "What? Really?"

I shook my head. "This is a conversation you need to be having with Burton, Luna. I'm just going on the record to let you know that, yes, he's into you."

Luna's eyes shone and she bit her lip. Then she took a deep breath and said briskly, "On to more interesting topics. I was hoping to hear how your date with Connor went last night. After I heard Connor might have a secret Ellie knew about, I almost asked you to let me know when you got back home safely."

I grimaced at the mention of the date and her eyes grew big. "That bad? What happened—did you end up with food poisoning?"

I was shaking my head and Luna guessed again. "Wait—did he stand you *up*?"

I realized this guessing game could potentially go on all day so I quickly intervened. "No, no. But you know how bad the weather was last night. Connor's car hydroplaned and we hit a ditch. It was a mess." I decided to keep my suspicions about Connor to myself until I found out more. After all, it was more of a gut feeling than anything else. Connor hadn't said he'd *dated* Ellie, only that he'd known her. Luna was already suspicious of him enough as it was.

"Ohh no." Then Luna frowned. "Doesn't he have that fancy sports car?"

Luna and I both drove old cars that could sometimes break down in spectacular and expensive ways, so I understood why she would ask the question. "Yes, but you know how it is when you hit a large puddle and you're going fast. Even though his car handles well under ordinary circumstances, it wasn't any match for the rain last night."

"But you're okay? Both of you? That must have scared you to death. Where did this happen?"

I made a face again. "That's what made it such a mess. Connor was planning this nice dinner for us so we were heading out of town and were in the middle of nowhere. It was going to take a little while for the tow truck to get to us." That was when I filled her in about Linus's involvement.

Luna clapped a hand over her heart. "That guy! He's the best. He even had Ivy with him?"

"He'd been taking her to the dog park when the weather turned," I said.

"So you and Connor took a rain check, I guess? No pun intended." Luna chuckled, regardless, at the pun.

I nodded but must have shown my lack of enthusiasm because Luna's voice dropped to a whisper and she said, "But you're not excited about it? Did anything else happen?"

I shrugged. "Not really. I don't know—I kind of felt like I was being railroaded last night. I'd had a long day at work and all I really wanted to do was curl up with Fitz."

"Yeah, but you do that every night, right? I thought the idea was that you were trying to get out of your shell a little."

"Oh, it is. Like I said, I've been trying to do more things, get out more. But I'm just not convinced Connor is the right guy to do those things with. I mean, it's good for me to push myself a little, but not great to feel like I wasn't being listened to," I said.

Luna said, "You mean you told him you didn't feel like going out and he was just dead-set on his own agenda?"

"Well, not totally like *that*. I didn't actually come out and tell him I didn't want to go out."

Luna put her hands on her hips. "That I believe. You don't like speaking up."

"I just realized he'd obviously put some time and energy into planning our evening, you know? He was all dressed up for one."

Luna made a face. "Which was probably even worse if you didn't want to go out in the first place. Were you still wearing your work clothes?"

"Even worse—I'd gone ahead and changed into something more casual because the clothes I'd worn here yesterday had gotten dusty when I was weeding out some old books from the collection."

Luna said, "So you were thinking you were going to just grab a casual meal with Connor."

"Something like that. Then I saw he had this romantic evening planned or something. I don't know—at least a *nice* evening even if it wasn't going to be a romantic one. I didn't want to disappoint him so I changed and we headed out. Then everything went downhill from there."

Luna quirked an eyebrow. "It wasn't just the weather?"

I hesitated. "I don't know, Luna. I just wasn't really getting the warm fuzzies last night. Like I said, it could have just been me and the mood I was in. But Connor was driving too fast and he's just so over-confident and sort of showy. I found it all really irritating." My voice dipped even lower than my already-low library voice. "It's totally wrong, but I keep comparing him to Grayson."

"Of course you do! Grayson is your crush."

I gave her a rueful look. "Yeah, but it's not like I'm in a relationship with him."

"Just give it time."

I snorted. "I've done nothing *but* give it time."

Luna glanced behind me and then her eyes opened wide again. "Don't look now, but Connor is coming straight over to this desk. I've just suddenly remembered I need to shelve some books."

Chapter Fifteen

Luna quickly scooted out and I took a deep breath. I really didn't feel like having any drama at work and I was being so productive and getting so much stuff knocked out. I didn't want anything to mess with my mojo.

I kept my head stubbornly down until I heard Connor softly saying my name. Then I looked up and gave a small smile. "Hey there," I said. "Did everything end up working out okay last night?"

Connor looked rueful. "Well, everything worked out as well as it possibly could, I guess. The car is being repaired at the shop and it's probably going to be expensive. But what I mostly wanted to do was to come by and apologize to you."

I sincerely hoped there wasn't going to be an invitation to dinner after work. I just needed a quiet evening by myself this time and was definitely going to make that clear this time *before* there was another date set up. Plus, I'd definitely worked myself up about Connor last night, right or wrong, and I didn't want to completely dismiss my gut reaction. Gut reactions exist for a reason.

"That's really not necessary," I said. "Accidents happen, right? All's well that ends well." I was, apparently, full of clichés when I was feeling awkward.

Connor shook his head and looked sad. "Unfortunately, it is necessary. I guess I've been on sort of a mission to impress you. Whether or not you want to be impressed."

"I don't need to be impressed. I just want to hang out," I said. I was still, apparently, a little tongue-tied but at least I thought the conversation was going in the direction I wanted it to. Except there was one more point I wanted to make. "You're my friend, Connor. We've been friends for a long while. Let's just go enjoy each other's company."

Connor slowly nodded. He'd clearly picked up on the "friend" part. "Got it. Of course. Anyway, I'm sorry about everything last night. You looked super-tired and I sort of dragged you out. I didn't pick a close place for us to go. Then I drove too fast for conditions." He gave me a small smile. "Maybe next time we should just meet at the restaurant and go out for burgers or something."

This was exactly what I needed to hear. But then, as I remembered from high school, Connor did seem to have a gift for saying the right thing when he needed to. That golden tongue of his had always seemed to get him out of tough spots when he got on the wrong side of a teacher. I said, "That sounds great. I'm sorry, too—sorry I wasn't great company last night. You're right—I was tired." I hesitated. "When I'm tired, I'm not a lot of fun. But you'd just come off a shift and were full of energy." I shook my head. "I'm not sure how you do that."

He snorted. "My mother would say it was my hyperactivity. That's just sort of how I am, I guess. When I've had a long day at work, I'm running on pure adrenalin. It takes a while for me to wind down and for it to wear off."

There was some movement behind Connor and I craned my neck to see around him, thinking it might be a patron who needed some help. But it was Grayson, carrying a backpack and looking thoughtfully at us.

Connor turned to see what I was looking at and then gave Grayson a toothy grin. He jutted out his hand. "I keep running into you, don't I? I'm Connor. I figure the universe is trying to tell us we need to meet each other."

Grayson's expression said that he very much doubted the universe had any such message for them. His face was somber as he carefully shook Connor's hand. "Grayson," he said briefly.

"Here to do some work?" I asked brightly. I felt there was a lot of underlying tension in the room and I couldn't really work out why. Grayson seemed to have taken an immediate dislike to Connor, no matter how charming Connor was to him.

Grayson nodded. "A little research on a town history piece I'm working on." He gave Connor a tight smile. "Hospital business bringing you here? Or are you here to check out books?" His tone seemed to suggest he found this highly unlikely.

Connor said lightly, "Oh, I might have Ann help me find something awesome to read while I'm here. I need to wind down a little after a long shift. But I'm mainly here to speak with her about our date last night."

I felt a flush rise up from my neck and settle in splotches on my face.

Grayson nodded stiffly and said, "Got it. Well, it was nice to meet you, Connor. I better head off and get this research done." He stalked off and I watched him thoughtfully.

Connor had already shifted back to focusing entirely on me again, which made me shift uncomfortably in my chair. "Anyway, I thought maybe I could make it up to you? Are you doing anything tonight after work?"

I immediately shook my head and said, "I need to have a quiet night tonight, Connor. I'm going to be as boring as I possibly can—it's going to be me, Fitz, a book, and a bowl of grits for supper."

There was a brief flash of irritation in Connor's face before he quickly gave me his winning smile again. "Got it. Well, I can't blame you. After last night, you're probably ready for something less exciting."

"I'm sorry how everything went last night. I hope your car will be okay."

He shrugged. "They seemed to think they could get it back to the condition it was in before. Anyway, that'll teach me to take it slower when the weather's bad." He gave me a rueful smile. Then he added, "I really don't even care about the car. I'm just glad you're okay. The car can be replaced. You can't."

This tempted the first real smile I'd given him that morning. When I glanced up, I saw Grayson was watching us from across the room before he quickly turned his focus back to the pile of books in front of him. "Thanks, Connor. Did you want me to give you some tips for things to read while you're here?"

"Tell you what—can you email some to me? I'm working my way through a book now that I'm not crazy about but I want to try to finish it. Maybe I can pick out one of your recommendations the next time I'm here."

"Sounds good," I said. "I keep a running list, so that will be easy enough."

"Why am I not surprised?" he asked, eyes twinkling.

I saw Pris, Ellie's sister, coming in the library door. She had her daughter with her—an absolutely adorable little girl with blonde pigtails. Pris raised her hand to wave with a smile and Connor said, "I'd better run and let you work. I'll call you soon, okay?"

I nodded and he left as Pris and her daughter came up to the desk.

"How are the two of you doing?" I asked.

"We gettin' books," the little girl murmured, putting a finger in her mouth and looking shy.

"Would you like to meet our library cat?" I asked her, looking up at Pris to make sure it was okay. Pris nodded.

The little girl's eyes grew big and she nodded solemnly. I glanced around and saw Fitz lying in a sunbeam and gave him a call. He immediately lifted his head and trotted our way. I came around the desk and stooped down next to Pris's daughter. "His name is Fitz," I said. "He loves to be petted. Here's how we're super-gentle with him."

I showed her how to pet him and the little girl gently scratched him under his chin until Fitz's whiskers quivered. He gave her a grateful look and bumped his furry head against her leg, making her giggle.

As she became absorbed in the cat, Pris said quietly, "Thank you, Ann. It's been something of a rough morning. I was looking for a way to distract Melissa after telling her about Ellie." She sighed. "I'm not sure I did the best job explaining that. But I'm still trying to figure it all out, myself."

"Of course you are," I said sympathetically. "Is Melissa here with you for a while?"

Pris shook her head sadly and said in a quiet voice, "No, just for one night. My ex-husband is taking her back tomorrow." She glanced at Melissa to make sure she wasn't listening and then added softly, "It breaks my heart every time she leaves. It's almost worse than not having her be here at all."

I saw Pris tear up and said quietly, "I'm so sorry. I really hope things start looking up for you soon."

She quickly swiped at her eyes with her sleeve and gave me a quick smile. "Thanks. It's been a rough year so far. I just keep thinking that the court is going to *have* to understand, right? A daughter needs her mother. I'm well-aware her father is better off financially, but surely they're going to take the emotional side of things into account."

"I'm sure they will," I said in a comforting voice, although I wasn't sure at all if that was the case.

Pris continued in her low, anxious voice, "My lawyer said the court wouldn't like the fact I moved away. But what else could I do? I didn't have a job when our marriage broke up. I didn't have any money independent of my husband and *he* wasn't going to provide me with any, that's for sure. I needed to move in with family and that meant Ellie. Ellie, bless her, took me in." Pris made a quick swipe at her eyes, pushing an errant tear away angrily.

"It was the most responsible thing to do," I said. "After all, I don't think the court would like it if you were homeless, right?"

"Exactly," said Pris eagerly. "That's exactly right. I was pushed into moving away. Pushed into dealing with these sudden, really dire circumstances. But I talked to my lawyer yesterday afternoon and now he says it's a problem that I don't have any 'family support' here in town, since Ellie is gone. He said my ex's lawyer is definitely going to bring up that I'm involved in a murder investigation. They're going to play all of this up. I really need this case to be solved quickly. I've been checking in with Burton every day."

"What has Burton told you?" I asked.

Pris shook her head, looking discouraged. "Either he doesn't know anything or can't say anything. I don't get a real feel for it, either way. I'm just worried my ex's lawyer is going to imply I'm somehow involved with Ellie's death. Or Frank's. That I'm a suspect or something."

"Do you think the police are treating you like a suspect?" I asked. I figured I actually knew the answer to this one—of course she was a suspect. She was living with Ellie. A murderer is quite often someone the victim knew really well. Like a family member. I knew Ellie and Pris had been squabbling with each other. "Were they asking about your alibi or anything?"

Pris glumly said, "I was at home during both of their deaths. The cops are acting like they're connected crimes. When Frank died, I was just boxing and bagging Ellie's stuff up. The problem with alibis is that you never know in advance when you might need one."

I said softly, "Again, I'm so sorry about Ellie's death. I know how close you two were. I wish I'd had a sister. It was sort of lonely being an only child."

Pris snorted and waved her hand dismissively. "Don't believe that she and I had the perfect relationship. As an only child, you might have an idealized view on siblings. Ellie could be hard to deal with. We fought like cats and dogs sometimes." She suddenly grew somber and said, almost to herself. "We had an argument the morning of the day Ellie died over something *so* stupid. I've been beating myself up over it. It just makes me feel so guilty that we were fussing over dumb stuff when I could have been enjoying the last time I ever saw her."

"Arguments happen," I said. "You had no idea that was going to be the last time with Ellie. It *shouldn't* have been the last time with Ellie."

"I guess. I wanted to borrow her car, that was all. She told me I was a bad driver and wouldn't let me borrow it." She snorted at this, but then gave a sob. "Like I said, it was always silly stuff with us."

Pris looked down at her daughter and ran a hand through her hair as she regained her composure. I said to the little girl, "Do you like Fitz?"

She turned her sweet face up to me and smiled. "He's so sweet."

I said, "Would you like me to take a picture of you two together?" I glanced at Pris to make sure this was okay and she nodded, looking pleased.

"Do you want me to take it with your phone? Or I can take it with mine and then email you the picture," I said.

Pris patted her pockets and looked rueful. "Typical me. I left my phone in the car. Do you mind emailing the picture?"

"Not a bit." I walked around the desk and squatted down, taking several pictures of Fitz and Melissa. I let Pris choose her favorite and then type in her email address and send it.

"Hope you both enjoy the library today," I said. "I bet Luna can help you find some great books."

A short while later, it was time for our tech drop-in. Like every first program, I was a little nervous, wondering if people would show up. But I needn't have worried—right before the event, there was a steady stream of patrons coming in with phones, tablets, and laptops and heading over to the computer room.

Then I was nervous wondering if Timothy had made it in. I probably could help out with a lot of the issues patrons had, as long as it was all fairly basic. But I'd feel a lot better if Timothy was there to navigate through the tougher issues.

I let out my pent-up breath in relief when I saw not only was he already in the computer room, he was helping a patron with an issue. He glanced up and gave me a grin and a wave when he saw me and I waved back at him. Then I started helping a woman who was having a problem logging in.

We actually had to run over a little bit because there were a couple of other people who'd come in later. I felt bad about having Timothy stay later than I'd said since he was just volunteering. But he was able to speedily fix the issues the patrons had and they left happy.

"Thanks so much for this," I said. "There's clearly no way I'd have been able to handle this event on my own. We ran over with two of us."

"No worries, I didn't mind. Besides, like I said, volunteering really looks good on my college applications and this is a different kind of volunteering than most students have. Anyway, it felt good to be able to help people. Most of the stuff was super-easy to fix."

I snorted. "Well, it probably seemed super-easy to you, but I bet it was an insurmountable problem to the people you were helping. They weren't able to get into their email or their social media or some of them even to log into their computer at all. So you were a huge help to them."

Timothy seemed to light up at the praise and was walking on cloud nine when he left the library. As he was leaving, Burton was coming inside. He walked up to me as I was finishing tidying up the computer area.

"How is everything going here?" he asked, looking around the library rather grimly as if expecting murderers to come leaping out at him any second.

"Much quieter than it has been," I said wryly. "The only excitement of the day was our tech repair drop-in event."

Burton nodded. "That's a good thing. Y'all have had way too much excitement around here and not the positive kind." He paused and asked casually, "How's Luna doing?"

I hid a smile. I was ready for Burton to finally take the plunge and ask Luna out. He'd been admiring her from afar for a long time but had always been hesitant to take the last step.

"You should go over to the children's section and ask her. I've been caught up in the tech drop-in and haven't really had a chance to spend time with Luna for a while."

Burton flushed a little and I continued, "You know how Luna is. You should just ask her to go to lunch with you or grab a coffee or something. She's so laid-back—she's not going to think anything of it."

Burton sighed. "That's exactly what I'm worried about—that she's not going to think anything of it."

"Well, you won't know if you don't try. It would give her the opportunity to see you in a different setting. She really only sees you *here*. Plus, she frequently only sees you when there's some sort of problem here at the library. It would be better for you to have a conversation with her when she wasn't at work . . . that way, she could see you in a different light."

Burton shook his head, making a face. "I don't want to really go out on a limb and invite her out unless I'm sure I won't get turned down."

"I *really* don't think she's going to say no. She might just think you're asking her to lunch as a friend, that's all."

"Yeah, that's what I'm afraid of," said Burton morosely.

"But that gives you the opportunity to turn it into something else, Burton. You can talk about things besides work."

Burton seemed to want to move on to other topics so I said, "How are things going with the cases?"

Burton shook his head. "They'd be going a whole lot better if people just told us the truth when we were asking them questions. Who knows—maybe Frank would still be alive if he'd just leveled with us."

I gave him a questioning look and he said, "Frank's alibi for the night of Ellie's death doesn't really pan out."

"Does that mean Frank killed Ellie? Then someone else killed Frank?" I frowned. I could definitely imagine Frank murdering Ellie because she threatened to expose him. But I had a harder time imagining someone killing Frank out of revenge for Ellie's death. Ellie didn't seem especially close to anyone—not close enough for someone to do that, anyway. Ted had been trying to back out of their relationship, from what he'd said. Pris, although it definitely seemed like she cared about her sister, didn't seem the type to be vengeful. At least not over her sister . . . her daughter might be a different story.

Burton said, "I'm not really sure if that's what it means or not. It could mean that while Frank was out and about that night, he saw something."

"Something that made him realize the identity of Ellie's killer?"

"Exactly. Frank's financial situation was shaky. In some ways he was sort of like Ellie—looking at blackmail as a way to make extra income."

We were suddenly interrupted by my phone ringing. I apologized and picked it up. Luna, who was at lunch, was on the other end and sounded breathless.

"Ann? Hey. My car finally broke down. I knew it was coming—it kept making all these crazy noises. Anyway, I'm stranded." She gave a slightly hysterical laugh. "It's starting to rain again and I'm supposed to be taking my mom to her physical therapy today. I'd call Wilson, but he's at a board meeting today."

I glanced across at Burton, who was oblivious. I said, "Unfortunately, I'm still scheduled to work until you come back in, but I've got an idea." I thrust the phone at Burton, who looked startled. I murmured, "Luna is stranded with car trouble and she and her mom need a lift to the doctor."

Burton quickly got on the phone. "Luna? Hi, it's Burton here. I'll pick you both up and take you to her appointment."

There was apparently surprise at the other end of the line. I could just barely hear Luna saying something about Burton going above and beyond his call of duty and then Burton said in his charmingly old-fashioned diction that always seemed to come out around Luna, "I'd be honored."

He handed the phone back to me and I put it to my ear. Luna sounded a little bemused. "Gosh, with a couple of murders, you'd think he wouldn't have time to help me out."

"You know Burton—always a gentleman," I said, smiling at Burton, who colored a bit.

After I hung up, I said sternly, "Be sure to make this time count! If she starts talking shop with you about the case, redirect her."

He grinned at me, looking sheepish as he made his way to the library exit. I had hit the nail on the head because Burton always lapsed into whatever was most comfortable for him to talk about when he was with Luna. Inevitably, this was work.

Chapter Sixteen

The next day, I realized maybe I needed to take my own advice. I was going on my hike with Grayson and definitely wanted to make the time with him count. I'd always carefully kept our conversations casual, preferring to comment about the landscape and less about anything of any consequence, mainly because that was my comfort level. And yes, I definitely talked about work from time to time.

The nice thing about going out somewhere with Grayson is there were no surprises. I know surprises are supposed to be these cool, fun things, but I'd never really enjoyed them. As boring as it was, I liked to pencil something in on my planner and know what to expect. I knew what we were going to do. I knew where we were going, and I knew what to wear.

So I put on my stretchy hiking pants and a cotton top with a light jacket in case it was breezy at the top of the mountain. That was it. I was completely ready. I had so much extra time that I decided to run by Keep Grounded and get a cup of coffee to go. It would also give me a great excuse to check in with Tara, who I really liked and hoped wasn't mixed up in all this.

The best thing about the coffeehouse, I decided, was that the coffee, while certainly more expensive than if I'd made a pot at home, wasn't outlandishly priced as long as I didn't get anything too fancy. Fortunately, it was quiet in there this time, too. So I ordered a large cup of regular coffee and then settled in to chat with Tara for a few minutes.

"How are things going?" I asked.

You could actually tell a lot about a person from the way they answered that very innocuous question. Most people, including myself, would answer 'fine.' But Tara seemed to look at it as an invitation to get a few things off her chest.

"Oh, it's okay. I had kind of a rough evening yesterday and ended up calling my sponsor to convince me I didn't need to drink or use drugs to get rid of my stress," said Tara with a sigh.

"But talking with your sponsor helped?" I asked.

"Oh yeah. She's an older woman and she's just so funny. It's hard to feel down when you're talking to her."

I took a sip of my coffee then said, "I'm sorry it was a rough day."

Tara shrugged. "You know, most of our customers here are awesome. But there were a few yesterday that were just so rude. Then Burton checked in with me again and I started worrying that I was going to somehow end up in jail." She glanced around as if a customer might somehow be listening in, but the place was completely deserted for once.

I shook my head. "I think Burton is checking in with *everybody*. He really wants these cases solved. Two murders in the space of a week in a small town is two murders too many in his book."

"Maybe." But Tara looked a little more cheerful.

I said, "The best bet is to try to give the police information that helps wrap the case up."

Tara said wryly, "I totally agree, but the problem is that apparently I know absolutely nothing. Which the police don't seem to really believe."

"I totally understand that. After all, we don't *know* when we're supposed to be paying attention. We're just working our job or out running errands and then suddenly someone needs to know what we've seen or heard. We may know nothing."

Tara rubbed her temple. "Exactly. I mean, the kind of stuff that I knew didn't even end up making any sense. I thought Frank had killed Ellie because she was blackmailing him. I knew about Frank's dark side. But that doesn't make any sense now in the context that Frank was murdered."

"And you didn't see anything the evening that Ellie was killed."

Tara gave a short laugh. "Well, I saw Frank out. Again—lots of evidence against Frank, which doesn't do us a lot of good. Besides, everybody was out that evening. I even thought I saw *Ellie* out the night she died."

I frowned. "Did you? Because she was on her own at the library that night." Would Ellie have left the library to run an errand or something? I quickly dismissed this idea. Ellie could definitely be irresponsible. But it was one thing to come back late from lunch and something totally different to leave the library unattended when no one else was working there.

"No, it wasn't her. It was her sister, driving her car. But she made me look twice, that's for sure."

I put my coffee cup down on the table, focusing all my attention on Tara. "That's funny. Ellie told Pris she couldn't drive her car that day."

Tara snorted. "Sounds like something my sister would say. Well, obviously she must have changed her mind. Pris doesn't even look that much like her sister—it was definitely her."

The bell rang on the door as a couple came in. I glanced at my watch. "Good catching up, Tara," I said quickly. "Take care of yourself."

Back at home, I grabbed my daypack, filled a water bottle, and poured my coffee into a thermos. I finished just in time as Grayson tapped on my front door.

"Hey there," he said lightly, leaning against the front door frame. "Got everything you need?"

"I think so. I'm kind of leaving the daypack packed up except for my water bottle to make sure I don't forget things. I even threw in an old pair of sunglasses that can just live in the bag."

He chuckled. "Threw them in there? It sounds like you afford your sunglasses about the same respect that I do. You must get cheap ones, like me."

I grinned back at him, feeling relaxed and happy. "Of course. I can't be trusted with nice sunglasses. I'd end up leaving them on the front seat of my car and then plopping down on top of them when I climb in. I don't deserve nice sunglasses, considering how I treat them."

Grayson smiled at me and I felt a frisson of warmth. We headed out in Grayson's car. I showed him a shortcut to the trail and we parked near the trailhead.

He glanced up the path as we climbed out. "Wow, that looks pretty steep. Glad I decided on my hiking boots today instead of my athletic shoes."

"Sorry . . . I should have told you. I'd forgotten it was this steep at the beginning. It does level off the more we go up, turning into a gradual incline. That's going to be something you'll want to point out to readers."

He nodded, tightening his laces and then gave me a teasing look. "Or maybe you were hoping to watch me stumble along?"

I shook my head with a laugh. Inside, my heart was thumping happily. Was it my imagination, or did Grayson seem to be flirting a little with me? We always had a nice, easy rapport . . . at least, we did after I stopped freezing up and falling all over myself when he was around me, but it never seemed quite *this* relaxed.

We made it up the steep incline without getting too winded. Just the same, it was nice to have the trail level off a bit and allow more conversation. We paused a few times so Grayson could take a couple of pictures for the newspaper—some fat blackberries, black-eyed Susans, and rhododendrons made for good photos for the accompanying article.

"How are things going at the paper?" I asked. At least this way I wasn't talking about *my* work, anyway.

"Surprisingly, it's going pretty well. Most newspapers are struggling right now because of print, but we've still got the same advertisers and the same subscribers that we had when I became the editor." He shrugged and gave me a smile, which gave me a warm flush. "I guess people in Whitby are creatures of habit."

"In every way," I said dryly. "I can totally believe that the subscribers wouldn't even consider stopping their subscription. After all, they've *always* subscribed. It would never occur to them to stop. Maybe we're all creatures of habit that way. I know my mornings have a very particular routine and so do my evenings. It's almost comforting to stay in the same patterns I always have. Although, lately, I have been trying to shake things up a bit."

A cloud crossed over Grayson's face. I wondered if I'd imagined it because he quickly turned away. Maybe he was frowning at the very healthy patch of poison oak that was looming on the side of the path. He said, "That can be a good thing, right? Pushing ourselves to do new things? With new people?" He paused. "It must be nice to reconnect with someone from your past like that."

I shrugged uncomfortably. "Oh, I don't know. I'm starting to think that Connor may not be the right choice for me to expand my borders with. He's just a little too unpredictable. He was probably just as unpredictable as he was when we were teenagers, but that was less of a problem for me back then. Or maybe I'm just a fuddy-duddy."

"You're definitely not a fuddy-duddy," said Grayson, sounding a little miffed on my account. "You just like things to happen in a particular way."

We walked on for a few more minutes, enjoying the cool breeze that was blowing down on us.

Grayson hesitated. "Do you enjoy music?" He added hurriedly, "It's just that there's a small concert that's coming up at the local theater soon. I was interested in going, but it's not as much fun going by myself. I'd enjoy it a lot more if I could talk about it with someone else."

I was watching him curiously. It wasn't like Grayson to stumble over his words like he was. It was more like *me*.

"Who's playing?" I asked. Then I laughed. "Actually, let me just take a flying leap for once. I *will* go. Thanks for asking. If my goal is to push myself more, I shouldn't even care who's playing."

Grayson relaxed a little. "It's a group called The Picket Fences. They were a college radio band while we were in college."

"I think I remember them," I said thoughtfully. "I used to hang out in school with some of the college radio DJs."

This moved our conversation into music and we discovered we had a lot in common with our musical tastes.

When we reached the top of the trail at the peak of the mountain, we stood for a few moments in silence, taking in the vista in front of us. The distant mountains rolled out ahead, creating that smudge of blue that gave the Blue Ridge Mountains their name.

Grayson again seemed a bit hesitant. "I know you just spoke about your love for routine, but I planned something a little different this time."

I watched as he opened up his backpack and removed a blanket and a small cooler with fruit and food inside. He grinned uncertainly at me.

"What a perfect idea," I said warmly.

And it was. We sat on the blanket, took in the view, and enjoyed his mini-banquet with a warm feeling of companionship between us. And, perhaps, something slightly more.

We reached for the potato salad at the same time and I felt a warm tingle as our hands brushed against each other. We laughed but I noticed Grayson didn't draw his hand away that quickly.

Grayson took some more photos before we left. I realized, if Grayson were indeed trying to make overtures, I may not seem to be making as many of my own. I hesitated. "Do you want to try some exercise again?" I chuckled. "Not that we haven't just struggled up a mountain, or anything. But it might be good to keep up the pace, at least for me. Maybe tomorrow? Just a light jog around the park?"

I immediately got the impression Grayson wanted to. "How flexible is your day tomorrow?" he asked. "I definitely would like to go, but I've got some work meetings and interviews planned, too."

"I'm off, so I can go whenever suits you best."

"Do you mind if we meet up first thing in the morning?" He made a face. "Sorry. I don't even know if you're a morning person. I hate to mess up your ability to sleep in on your day off, but one of my meetings is over dinner tomorrow, so that's going to run late."

"That's perfect," I said with a smile. "I have to get up early for work every day, so when I'm off, I'm still on that same routine. Besides, if I sleep in too long, Fitz will make little hints that he would like to be fed."

He grinned at me. "I bet that's cute."

"It is cute," I admitted. "He'll snuggle right up against my face on my pillow and purr loudly. If I'm still comatose, he'll pat his paw super-gently against my face to get my attention. You'd think it would be a little irritating, but he's so careful and gentle that it always just wakes me slowly up."

Grayson was thinking about getting a puppy, so we talked about that for a while as we finished up our picnic, packed up our trash, and then started heading slowly back down the mountain. I realized again how different it was being out with Grayson than Connor. I felt really energized right then, despite having had a pretty strenuous hike. When I was out with Connor, it wasn't that I was *exhausted*, but more that I could feel my energy being depleted. It wasn't that I didn't like him, it was just that his energy seemed to sort of dominate mine.

After Grayson had driven me home, he gave me a warm smile. "Hey, thanks for doing this with me, Ann. I'll see you tomorrow morning." He watched me as I walked into my house before driving away.

It was something to look forward to.

Later that day, I headed out to the grocery store to finally make some headway on restocking my fridge and shelves. The store was right next to the little vegetarian deli where Luna and I sometimes ate. Sitting outside under an umbrella, was Connor with a woman I recognized from around town, but didn't know.

Connor spotted me and stood up, looking embarrassed. "Ann," he said.

I smiled and walked over. "Hi, Connor," I said cheerfully. In some ways, it sort of amused me to see him looking so uncomfortable since he was always so collected.

He quickly introduced me to his friend who gave me a cool smile in return.

"Well, good to meet you. And good to see you, Connor." I walked to the grocery store and went in.

I wasn't surprised when, sometime after supper, Connor called me. His voice was penitent on the other end. "Hi, Ann. Sorry about all that today. She and I were just having lunch together."

"Connor, you don't have to explain yourself to me. We're not tied to each other, after all. You're free to have lunch with anyone you choose."

Connor said in a persistent tone, "But I'd like to be tied down, Ann. I love spending time with you."

"I like spending time with you, too. But the truth is I think you and I are just too different to make things work. We want different things." Plus, I had to admit I was feeling conflicted about Connor's possible connection to Ellie.

Connor said, "What do you mean?" His voice indicated he thought I might be making some sort of subtle dig at him and his priorities when that wasn't true.

"It's just that I'm used to a pretty set routine and like a lot of quiet time. Connor, I think I'd probably bore you to death after a while. Right now our relationship is still new and all the faults and cracks haven't really shown up yet. It wouldn't take long for you to want something or someone a little more exciting."

Connor was quiet for a few moments, absorbing this. Then, apparently, he was willing to accept it. Maybe, after all, he had been attracted to the woman he was having lunch with—maybe he was already wanting a relationship that wasn't quite as quiet. Then he said, "All right, Ann. But if it's all right with you, I'd like to be friends. Maybe we can sometimes do things together as friends?"

I chuckled. "This town is way too small for us to feel uncomfortable around each other. We'd simply keep endlessly running into each other if we're not friends. Besides, there aren't too many people in Whitby who've known me most of my life."

Connor sounded relieved. "Great! All right, I'll make sure to call you up for a coffee or a drink at some point soon."

That settled, Connor made his goodbyes and hung up. I couldn't help but wonder if he was getting right back on the phone again to schedule dinner with the woman he'd had lunch with.

The next morning, *I* was the one giving Fitz little snuggly rubs to wake him up. He gave me a disbelieving look since it was still dark outside and even earlier than it would have been if I'd been getting ready for work.

My phone rang and I frowned, craning my neck to look at the screen while I was scraping Fitz's breakfast into a bowl.

"Hi, Wilson," I said, cradling the phone between my shoulder and ear as I plopped the bowl of cat food in front of Fitz and watched as he enthusiastically ate it up.

Wilson greeted me and said, "Sorry about calling you on your day off."

I told him it was no big deal. But the reason it wasn't a big deal is because Wilson frequently did call me on my off-days. It was fine—he was usually very brief. It always seemed like he had something on his mind and needed to contact me *right then* to bounce it off.

"We're getting quite a few messages and calls from people asking when the next tech drop-in is," he said. "I've been looking on our calendar and I don't see one scheduled."

"Really? Wow, okay. Well, as you know, there was a good deal of turnout for our first one. Maybe word has spread or maybe the folks who attended have even *more* tech problems with different devices. I don't have a day set up yet. Because of the volume, I really need to have Timothy there with me to help out."

Wilson said in his measured voice, "Is he amenable to that?"

"Definitely. He talked about it being a unique way to get volunteer work in for school and it ties in to experience for his future plans, since he wants to go into IT. But I need to check with him and find out some good dates. I may just go ahead and schedule the next two or three, if possible. Then I can advertise them on social media."

Wilson said, "All right. Let me know if you run into any issues with finding good dates and maybe the library can pay for our new tech contractor to help out. I hate for patrons to call in and not be able to tell them any scheduled dates for the next event." He sighed. "I certainly hope this new contractor will prove to know what he's talking about. He's coming in today. At least he may not end up murdered, like Frank."

I bit my lip to keep from chuckling. Wilson was making it sound as if Frank had been supremely irresponsible to end up murdered. Although, perhaps, he was.

"You know," said Wilson thoughtfully, "I intended on speaking with Frank before his untimely demise. I wanted to afford him the opportunity to respond to the allegations against him. He was at the library on one of your days off and when I walked over to talk to him, he was on a call with someone. It sounded to me like he was engaged in some scurrilous activity. At last, it was certainly *unprofessional* activity."

I could tell Wilson was bristling on the other end at the memory. "What was the conversation?" I asked. "Could you hear what he was talking about?"

"Frank was pressuring someone on the phone. It was quite clear. Frank said, 'I know you're selling pills. If you want me to keep quiet about it, you're going to have to pay.' That's when I stopped listening."

My mind was whirling. Was Frank speaking to someone who wasn't one of the current suspects? Or could he possibly have been speaking with Tara? As far as I knew, though, she'd only been taking pills and hadn't been selling them. I knew that taking using into the realm of selling became a completely different thing in the eyes of the law.

"What did you do then?" I asked.

Wilson sighed a heavy sigh on the other end. "Well, I didn't want to give him the chance to defend himself right then. I decided to just call him after he'd finished the job that day and inform him I was ending the contract. He was suspected of abusing his wife and I heard him blackmailing someone. That was enough for me. But I never had the chance to do it because I got caught up with other tasks and then he was dead." He must have looked at his watch because he said briskly, "I'll let you go now, Ann. If you'll just let me know when you get in touch with Timothy and have a date set for the tech drop-in?"

And he hung up.

I glanced at the clock as I was leaving and realized I was way too early to meet Grayson at the park. I decided to run by Keep Grounded first and see Tara. I hoped there was a good way to broach the subject of what Wilson had overheard.

When I walked into the coffee shop, it was completely dead inside. Tara was busily getting things ready behind the counter—putting out fresh muffins and croissants. She smiled when she saw me walk in.

"Ann! Good to see you," she said. "You're in here early."

I grinned at her. "I'm an early riser, but usually I just go right to the library. It's my day off today, so I'm heading for the park to take a run, but I thought maybe I'd slide by here first and get some fuel for exercising.

Tara got me set up with a large cup of regular coffee and then came around to join me at a table for a few minutes. "How is everything going with you?" she asked. "How are things at the library?"

I said, "It's been good over there, and a little different without Ellie there."

"I'm sure it has been," said Tara snorting. "You don't have to worry about someone listening in on your conversations anymore."

There was a bit of sharpness in her tone, but I couldn't really blame her. After all, she'd trusted Ellie as a friend—confiding in her. Then Ellie had used her trust against her to try and extort money from her. That would be upsetting for anybody.

I said, "Well, and we could also use some more help over there. The library has been really busy lately, which is great, but a couple of extra hands would really make a difference."

"Any news from Burton or anybody about the case?" asked Tara.

I shook my head. "No one's been arrested, at least. I'm hoping the police are a lot closer to figuring things out." I paused. "There's one thing that's been on my mind that I wanted to ask you about. Somebody mentioned to me that you'd been selling pills—I guess the painkillers you'd been on? You know how things are in small towns—stuff gets so distorted."

A look of irritation flashed over Tara's features. "I've never been a drug dealer in my life. But I've been an *addict*. That's something I freely admit to. Now I've turned my life around, but people still won't let you forget. It makes it really hard for me to move forward when folks in town are always looking at me and thinking about what I used to be like."

"You're proving them all wrong," I said smoothly, realizing this was a sore spot for her. I was about to move on and start talking about more pleasant subjects when Tara cut in.

"Besides, you shouldn't have listened to anything Frank said. You know the kind of person he was."

I said, slowly, "I didn't say it was Frank who mentioned it to me."

Chapter Seventeen

Tara paled. Then she lunged, enraged, at me. Taken by surprise, I fell and tried to scramble back up, but Tara kicked me. I was trying to remember my self-defense moves that Burton had taught me some time ago, but was so taken off guard that I ran behind the counter since Tara was between me and the door. Tara followed me and as I desperately looked for something to use as a weapon, she swung a heavy blender at me. I ducked at the last second, then, belatedly, remembered my pepper spray. I pulled it from my pocket and held my arm out straight, emptying out a steady stream of fluid that hit her square in the eyes.

Tara let out a roar and grabbed at her face. I didn't wait around to see what happened next—I took off running to the door and out toward my car, dialing Burton as I went. Gasping, I quickly explained the situation.

Burton was on it. I could hear the faint sounds of a siren some distance away. I turned around to check on Tara and saw her stumbling furiously in my direction.

The siren was still some distance away, so I glanced around my car for a weapon of some kind to use on Tara to keep her from running off. I figured I'd pretty much emptied the pepper spray so I didn't want to try it again.

I was just reaching for the less-than-ideal insulated water bottle I had in the car, thinking I could swing it at Tara when I heard a shriek and a thump and saw Tara had dashed out in front of a car and was lying on the ground as the car screeched to a halt.

Connor, white-faced, rushed out of the vehicle and crouched next to Tara on the ground. "Are you all right?" he asked intently, checking Tara gently for injuries. "You jumped out right in front of me."

Tara was woozy and trying to get her breath. I saw her eyes look wildly around as Burton's police car finally pulled up to a screeching stop. Grayson, brow furrowed with concern, pulled in just seconds afterward.

Tara looked like the fight had totally gone out of her. She pushed herself up to a sitting position and pushed at Connor as he still tried to examine her. Burton hopped out of the car and hurried over.

"What happened?" Burton asked grimly as Grayson walked up to us. Grayson asked if I was okay in a low voice and I nodded shakily.

Connor said roughly, "I spotted Ann's car in the parking lot and was pulling in to the coffee shop just to say hi and grab some caffeine before my shift starts. This woman ran right in front of me. We should call an ambulance."

"I don't need an ambulance," said Tara fiercely. "You just knocked the wind out of me, that's all."

Burton said, "I'm calling one anyway, just to be on the safe side."

"Great. So you don't even believe me," said Tara.

Burton quirked an eyebrow as if to say that the situation and the woman before him didn't really warrant believing.

He made the phone call and then briskly hung up.

Connor checked his watch and quickly said, "I've got to head to work. I'll talk to you later, Ann."

Burton asked Grayson to wait outside the coffee shop and then locked the door and sat down at a table with me and Tara.

Burton said, "Now, let's talk about what happened."

Tara was silent, so I said, "Tara realized she'd given herself away as the killer. She attacked me and I sprayed her with pepper spray."

Sure enough, Tara's eyes were still red and watering from the spray and she gave them a resentful swipe.

Burton informed Tara of her rights as she continued swabbing at her face.

"Could I give her my water bottle?" I asked Burton. "Just to flush her eyes out?"

Burton nodded as he took out a small notebook. We watched as Tara both caught her breath and washed out her eyes.

In his steady way, Burton said, "Tara, it's all over. You don't have to run anymore. Could you fill me in and tell me what happened?"

Tara started rocking in her chair in a self-comforting movement. Then she looked up at me, eyes red from the spray. "Ann, I'm sorry. I really like you."

Strangely, this apology was totally acceptable to me. She was apologizing for trying to kill me just a few short minutes ago, but I know she didn't want to. It made it easier to forgive, although I wouldn't forget. I gave her a reassuring nod and waited to see if Tara would fill us in or whether she was going to ask for a lawyer, instead.

But the desperate instinct to fight that had been so evident when she was swinging the blender at me was gone and now she was just crumpling inside herself. She took a deep, shuddering breath. "I never wanted any of this to happen."

"Of course you didn't," said Burton, still in that soothing, concerned voice.

He seemed to give Tara some strength to keep going. She gave him a grateful look and straightened back up a little in her chair. "When I got hooked on prescription drugs, everything went downhill fast. Before that, I had goals and I knew where I was heading. I knew I had a future ahead of me. But the drugs took all of it away from me until all I cared about was getting more drugs."

Burton nodded. "They hook you that way."

"They keep you from thinking for yourself," said Tara, bitterly. "Normally, I think I'd be able to see through somebody like Ellie. I mean, she wasn't ever going to be a real friend to me. She was looking out for *herself*. But when I was using, I couldn't see that. It was so obvious. I never would have been friendly with her if I'd been my normal self."

Tara made her actions sound reasonable, but I couldn't forget that she'd killed . . . twice. I kept my voice calm as I noted, "Ellie was good at manipulating people, from what I could tell.

You shouldn't blame yourself too much for not realizing she was trouble. I think she was trying to dupe people into telling her their secrets. Pris mentioned Ellie was thinking of starting her own business. I wonder if blackmailing *was* the business."

Tara gave a sad smile. "Maybe I shouldn't blame myself, like you're saying. Just the same, trusting Ellie led me down a dark path, didn't it? I told you a little about it, Ann. I'd confided everything to Ellie because I was trying to borrow some money from her." She snorted. "Borrow. Yeah. That money definitely wouldn't have been paid back to her because at that point I was addicted and just looking to get more pills. Anyway, she turned against me and started blackmailing me."

Burton nodded. "But then you switched jobs and cleaned yourself up. There's no way you're faking being clean right now."

It was true—Tara seemed to be in great shape, aside from the red, pepper-sprayed eyes. She didn't look like a user. But why had she been selling pills?

Tara replied, "Yeah, I'm clean. But I made one final mistake. I'd just paid the rest of my money for the pills I had on hand. I wanted to get rid of the pills so I wouldn't be tempted to take them. But I didn't want to just flush them down the toilet, either. I needed a little money to carry me through until I got my first paycheck from the coffeehouse. So I sold them to somebody else." She looked sort of sick as she said this, whether from guilt or from the moment she'd sealed her own fate, I wasn't sure.

"How did Ellie find out you were selling?" I asked softly.

Tara gave a harsh laugh. "I sure didn't tell her, if that's what you're thinking. I'd already learned my lesson about confiding in Ellie. No, she actually knew the guy I was selling to and he mentioned it to Ellie offhandedly, apparently. He was an ex-boyfriend of hers, but they were still in touch. Ellie told me he fed her information and then she paid him a cut of what she made from blackmailing her victims." Tara shook her head. "She was proud of it like she'd started her own business."

"Which she had," said Burton wryly. "Just not a legitimate one. Okay, so obviously Ellie tried to blackmail you again. The first time hadn't worked because you just ended up quitting your job at the hospital before you got fired and then cleaning your-self up so she didn't have anything to blackmail you *over*. This time, you figured you needed to fix your problems another way."

Tara nodded miserably. "I didn't want to. But you don't know how persistent Ellie was. She wasn't going to leave it alone. I told her I didn't *have* any money, which was the truth. That was the whole reason I'd sold the pills, just to make my rent until I got my first paycheck at Keep Grounded. But she told me I could ask my parents or my sister for money." Her face was cold at the memory. "There was no way I was going to do that."

"You ended up at the library before it closed the night you killed Ellie. Was that planned between the two of you? Or did you show up there?" asked Burton.

Tara took another deep, shuddering breath. "It wasn't planned. I wanted to see if anyone was at the library before I went in there. Obviously, I wanted Ellie alone."

"So you drove over there during your shift, apparently. Be-cause you were working."

Tara said quickly, "I just walked there and back. I didn't want anyone to see my car gone. I taped a sign to the coffeehouse door and said I'd be back soon, but nobody came by, apparently. I hurried over there. It was very dark."

"When you got to the library, what did you see?"

Tara said, "Well, I saw Pris dropping off Ellie's car. I waited for her to leave and she did—she hurried out of the parking lot and set off down the street like she was walking home. I guessed that was where she was going, anyway."

"What time was this?" I asked.

"It was about 8:30. Pris obviously wanted to get the car there and get back home before Ellie left work." Tara shrugged. "At least, that's what I figured. She looked really furtive like she didn't want anyone to see her. I guessed she'd borrowed the car without permission or something."

Burton asked grimly, "What happened when you went inside the library?"

Tara said, "Ellie assumed I was there to pay up. I told her again that I didn't have any money, but she wasn't going to stop. I gave her another chance to give me a break—I asked again to just drop the whole thing. But she laughed and turned her back on me to shelve books. She just kept running her mouth, talking about how I was going to end up in jail. I walked around to the other side of the shelves."

Burton raised his eyebrows. "And she didn't see you."

"She was too busy trying to make digs at me. Plus, she was on the end of the shelving and I was in the center, so I wasn't directly in front of her. I shoved." Tara's voice became quieter. "That was it."

"That was a huge bookshelf to topple," said Burton.

Tara shrugged again. "I was furious."

This made me shiver. It must have been an explosive anger indeed to fuel Tara into shoving down that shelving.

Burton jotted down a few notes into the small notebook he carried. Then he said, "Tell us about Frank."

Tara said, "When I left the library, there was no one around. But when I was driving out of the parking lot, I saw another car going by. I didn't know who was driving it and didn't think it was a big deal until Frank came by the coffee shop one morning and told me he knew what I'd done." Her voice was steely.

"He'd been the one who saw you leave," I said.

"*He* planned to blackmail me." Tara gave a short laugh and shook her head. "Frank didn't realize this was exactly why I'd had to kill Ellie. I couldn't seem to get away from low-life scum in this town. I told him the same thing—I didn't have the money. He said he'd just go to the police, then." She held out her hands. "All I've been trying to do is to turn my life around and start back on the right path. I never asked for any of this to happen."

"So what happened next?" asked Burton.

"I told Frank I had information on *him*, too. That I knew he'd been responsible for his wife's death. That if he went to the police then I'd head to the police, too." She shook her head. "But he said the only thing I had on him was hearsay and wouldn't be taken seriously by the police. Ellie was dead and she was the one who'd spoken directly to his wife."

"He wasn't going to drop it," I said.

"Exactly," said Tara. "So I told him not to go to the police, that I would be able to come up with some sort of payment for him. He asked me to meet him out at the lake. When I got there,

I killed him." She swallowed. "But do you see how I didn't really have a choice?" Her voice was pleading.

Burton didn't answer her. "Why did you attack Ann?"

Tara sighed, looking down at the floor. "I didn't want to. Like I said, I didn't have a choice. She'd figured it out—found out about me selling pills. I didn't want to hurt her."

Burton nodded, making a few last notes before standing up. "Tara, it's time for us to head to the station."

I walked out behind them and met up with Grayson.

"Remember," called Burton behind him to Grayson. "None of this goes into the paper yet. I'll call you later to give you a statement for tomorrow's edition, okay?"

"Sounds good," said Grayson.

We watched as Tara was loaded into the backseat of the police cruiser and Burton drove away.

Grayson looked at me with concern. "Ann, are you okay?"

I gave a shaky chuckle. "Let's just say I don't think I'm up for that run after all."

"Of course you're not. Do I need to call anybody for you? A friend? It looks like Connor won't be available." Grayson's mouth twisted when he said Connor's name, as if it tasted bad in his mouth.

"No. No, I think I'll be just fine here with you," I said.

"I'm guessing you don't want to go somewhere else for a coffee, but how about breakfast?" Grayson asked, still looking at me worriedly.

I shook my head. "No, thanks. I think I'd rather be at home." I took a deep breath and took the plunge. "Would you like to come over? I actually have some pretty decent coffee there.

Maybe I can round up a little food in the fridge. I think I have eggs."

Grayson looked surprised, then pleased. "Me? Sure, that sounds great—thanks."

We headed towards our cars and our eyes met one final time. His gaze lingered, and he cracked another smile. A real one. Despite the chaos of the last few minutes, for one bliss-filled moment, it felt like we were the only two people around.

About the Author:

Elizabeth writes the Southern Quilting mysteries and Memphis Barbeque mysteries for Penguin Random House and the Myrtle Clover series for Midnight Ink and independently. She blogs at ElizabethSpannCraig.com/blog, named by Writer's Digest as one of the 101 Best Websites for Writers. Elizabeth makes her home in Matthews, North Carolina, with her husband. She's the mother of two.

Sign up for Elizabeth's free newsletter to stay updated on releases:

https://bit.ly/2xZUXqO

This and That

I love hearing from my readers. You can find me on Facebook as Elizabeth Spann Craig Author, on Twitter as elizabethscraig, on my website at elizabethspanncraig.com, and by email at elizabethspanncraig@gmail.com.

A special thanks to John DeMeo and Karen Young for their support!

Thanks so much for reading my book...I appreciate it. If you enjoyed the story, would you please leave a short review on the site where you purchased it? Just a few words would be great. Not only do I feel encouraged reading them, but they also help other readers discover my books. Thank you!

Did you know my books are available in print and ebook formats? Most of the Myrtle Clover series is available in audio and some of the Southern Quilting mysteries are. Find the audiobooks here.

Please follow me on BookBub for my reading recommendations and release notifications.

I have Myrtle Clover tote bags, charms, magnets, and other goodies at my Café Press shop: https://www.cafepress.com/cozymystery

If you'd like an autographed book for yourself or a friend, please visit my Etsy page.

I'd also like to thank some folks who helped me put this book together. Thanks to my cover designer, Karri Klawiter, for her awesome covers. Thanks to Freddy Moyano for the concept! Thanks to my editor, Judy Beatty for her help. Thanks to beta readers Amanda Arrieta and Dan Harris for all of their helpful suggestions and careful reading. Thanks to my ARC readers for helping to spread the word. Thanks, as always, to my family and readers.

Other Works by Elizabeth:

Myrtle Clover Series in Order (be sure to look for the Myrtle series in audio, ebook, and print):

Pretty is as Pretty Dies

Progressive Dinner Deadly

A Dyeing Shame

A Body in the Backyard

Death at a Drop-In

A Body at Book Club

Death Pays a Visit

A Body at Bunco

Murder on Opening Night

Cruising for Murder

Cooking is Murder

A Body in the Trunk

Cleaning is Murder

Edit to Death

Hushed Up

A Body in the Attic

Murder on the Ballot

Death of a Suitor (2021)

Southern Quilting Mysteries in Order:

Quilt or Innocence

Knot What it Seams

Quilt Trip

Shear Trouble

Tying the Knot

Patch of Trouble

Fall to Pieces

Rest in Pieces

On Pins and Needles

Fit to be Tied

Embroidering the Truth

Knot a Clue

Quilt-Ridden (2021)

The Village Library Mysteries in Order (Debuting 2019):

Checked Out

Overdue

Borrowed Time

Hush-Hush

Where There's a Will (2021)

Memphis Barbeque Mysteries in Order (Written as Riley Adams):

Delicious and Suspicious

Finger Lickin' Dead

Hickory Smoked Homicide

Rubbed Out

And a standalone "cozy zombie" novel: Race to Refuge, written as Liz Craig

Printed in Great Britain
by Amazon